LOVE AT EMBURY COURT

Jenny, a young teacher in London, spends her long summer holiday at Embury Court, a beautiful Tudor mansion where her uncle is curator. Also in residence are the handsome son and heir of the owners, Lord and Lady Mountfields, and an artist employed to paint romantic views of the house to sell in the souvenir shop. Between the two of them, and the vagaries of the weather, Jenny is whirled on to a merry-go-round of love, laughter, danger and tears.

Books by Beryl Walthew
in the Linford Romance Library:

HIDEAWAY HOUSE
A PLACE TO DREAM

BERYL WALTHEW

LOVE AT EMBURY COURT

Complete and Unabridged

LINFORD
Leicester

First published in Great Britain in 1992 by
Robert Hale Limited
London

First Linford Edition
published 2001
by arrangement with
Robert Hale Limited
London

British Library CIP Data

Walthew, Beryl
    Love at Embury Court.—Large print ed.—
Linford romance library
    1. Love stories
    2. Large type books
    I. Title
    823.9′14 [F]

ISBN 0–7089–4570–8

Published by
F. A. Thorpe (Publishing)
Anstey, Leicestershire
Set by Words & Graphics Ltd.
Anstey, Leicestershire
Printed and bound in Great Britain by
T. J. International Ltd., Padstow, Cornwall

This book is printed on acid-free paper

1

'Jenny dear, would you mind very much giving up your trip to Greece with your friends?' asked Mrs Collins, looking up from her letter with a worried frown.

'It wouldn't break my heart exactly,' answered her daughter cheerfully. 'Why?'

'Your Aunt Sarah has broken her leg in two places, so now of course she's in plaster and can't move.'

'The poor old girl! How did she do that?'

'She doesn't seem to know. Twisted her ankle somehow and fell down the terrace steps. It's those ridiculous high heels she will insist on wearing. I'm always telling her they're dangerous.'

'Well, she has to dress the part of Lady of the Manor,' laughed Jenny.

'But she's not the Lady of the Manor, she's only the wife of the

1

caretaker,' snapped her mother with sisterly venom.

'Curator, Mother, not caretaker. Don't be catty. But what's it all got to do with me?'

'She wants you to go down to Embury Court and help cope with the tourists. It's a bit much to ask, but you are the only one of the family with a long summer holiday.'

'Relax, Mother! Of course I'll go. You know I love Embury!'

'Thank you dear. That is good of you. I'll write to Sarah straight away and put her mind at rest. She's lucky to have such a kind and helpful niece.'

'Oh, for heaven's sake, Mother, don't invest me with a halo! I shall enjoy it at Embury. It'll be my turn to play the Lady of the Manor. As a matter of fact I shall be glad of the excuse to get away from the mob. I see them every day!'

'Tim will be upset though, won't he?'

'He'll live,' replied her daughter with the callousness of a pretty girl who has never lacked for male attention.

Jenny lived with her widowed mother in the London suburb of Northcote and was a teacher at the local primary school, where staff and children alike were looking forward eagerly to the holidays. It had been a gruelling term as summer terms always are, with school fête and sports, examinations to be marked, reports to be written and parents to be interviewed. But first she had the painful task of telling her friends that her plans had altered.

Her fellow teachers, Norah and Sally, accepted her decision calmly but Tim Brown, the games specialist, was furious. He had been hoping that the romantic Isles of Greece would soften her heart towards him.

'It's too bad of you to upset all our arrangements like this!' he expostulated. 'Anyway you can't do it. The tickets are booked.'

'I shall plead family illness and get my money back,' replied Jenny calmly.

'That's all very well, but you're leaving us in the lurch.'

'I'm sorry Tim, but I just have to go to Embury. I'm needed there.'

'You're needed with us. If you don't come it will put the whole party out of gear.'

'Of course it won't! Sally's husband is going so that makes a foursome. An ideal arrangement.'

'You don't give a damn about me do you?'

'Oh please, Tim, don't start all that again! Why don't you team up with Norah? She thinks a lot of you and she'll be much kinder to you than I am.'

'She could hardly be worse,' growled Tim.

'I'm sorry you're upset,' said Jenny, 'but I can't stand here arguing all day. I've got work to do. My class will be in an uproar.'

She escaped with relief into her classroom and quickly forgot Tim and his troubles in the demands of her pupils.

The term seemed to drag on endlessly, until at last the final day came. When the children had departed with much laughter and excitement, and the building had ceased to re-echo with their youthful hubbub, the teachers were sitting in the staff-room in various attitudes of exhaustion. While they tried to pull themselves together with the aid of a bottle of cheap sherry, they regaled each other with their holiday plans.

Most were making for the Mediterranean and the sun. The Headmaster, richer than the rest, was off to Florida, but the Deputy Head, a family man with a large brood, could afford nothing more exotic than a caravan at Ramsgate.

'I shall be staying at Embury Court,' announced Jenny smugly.

Tim Brown sat glowering in a corner, but the others pricked up their ears with interest.

'Embury Court! Do you mean that magnificent Tudor mansion in Dorset?' exclaimed the Head.

'Yes, that's the one.'

'I went over it last year. It was most

impressive. The pictures alone must be worth millions.'

'Yes they are.'

'Doesn't it belong to Lord Mountfields?' asked Mrs Johnson, the school secretary. 'Do you know him?'

'Of course I know him.'

'Good grief, she's in with nobs!' cried Sheila, the Head of the Infants Department. 'Didn't Princess Margaret stay at Embury a few years ago? Do we have to curtsey to you?'

'Yes I think you should,' teased Jenny. 'I promise to be gracious.'

'Oh come off it Jenny!' intervened her close friend, Norah, who knew the truth. 'Tell them the whole story, we're all too tired to play games.'

Jenny laughed and relented.

'You can all relax,' she said. 'My uncle is curator of the historic treasures at Embury. I'm going there to help my aunt with the tourists. I'm only a worm to Lord Mountfields, I doubt if he'll even notice me.'

'Let's all make up a party and go

down to Embury to see her,' suggested Norah mischievously.

'If you do you'll each have to pay five pounds entrance fee, and buy your own teas in the cafeteria and that's not cheap,' warned Jenny.

'I don't think she wants us to visit her,' joked the Head. 'I do believe she's up to something.'

'That's it. Of course she's up to something!' said Norah. 'Look at her! There's guilt written all over her. Lord Mountfields is well known to be a lecher!'

'Rubbish!' cried Jenny, flushing indignantly. 'He's a harmless old boy, only interested in horses.'

'No, it's his son who's the wild one,' said Mrs Johnson. 'He was had up in court at Cambridge for throwing a wild party and being drunk and disorderly.'

'That's all newspaper talk,' scoffed Jenny. 'You shouldn't read the gutter press. Anyway he won't look at me. He's probably surrounded by bimbos.'

'You'd better be careful all the same,'

warned Miss Simmonds, the elderly doyenne of the staff-room. 'You can't trust the nobility, they're too used to getting their own way.'

'Whatever have you been reading?' jeered Jenny. 'A *True Confessions* magazine?'

'You mark my words, madam,' said Miss Simmonds, bridling. 'Many a girl has wished she hadn't laughed at her elders. I'll tell you that for nothing.'

Jenny glanced round at her fellow teachers. They had all twisted their faces into a look of solemnity in the effort not to snigger.

'Of course I'm not laughing at you, Simmy dear,' she said. 'I promise to avoid all high-class wolves like the plague.'

Miss Simmonds did not realize that her awful warnings only made Jenny all the more eager to meet this dangerous young aristocrat.

That being the case she had no time for poor Tim Brown when he tried to intercept her on her way out.

'Cheerio, Tim! Have a good time in Greece. See you in September,' she said and departed smartly.

As she walked home she could not help feeling a pang of guilt at the way she had treated her devoted swain.

'It was time I put paid to that lad,' she reassured herself. 'He was getting too possessive. Norah will be just what the doctor ordered for him.'

Early the next morning, refreshed by the sound sleep of youth, Jenny was ready to set out for Embury.

'Be sure and phone me the moment you get there,' fussed her mother. 'And do drive carefully. The roads are so dangerous these days.'

'Of course I shall drive carefully. I always do. Now stop worrying,' said Jenny, kissing her.

'And be sure and give Sarah my love, and tell her I hope she'll soon be about again,' said Mrs Collins for the umpteenth time.

'Yes Mother, I shan't forget. Now I really must start if I want to get there before dark. Goodbye Mother. Be good.'

With a final cheerful wave, Jenny dumped her case into the back of her battered old mini, clambered in and turned its nose towards Dorset. She sang as she left the stuffy town behind her and sped down the motorway. She was young, heart-whole and fancy free, and she had seven weeks of respite from the hurly burly of the classroom to look forward to.

'One little maid from school, that's me,' she warbled.
'Perto-n-fierce as a school-marm well may be.
Full to the brim with girlish glee-hee!
One little maid from school.'

Her brave little car seemed to purr beneath her feet.

'Tiddly, tiddly, tiddly tum,' said Jenny. 'Embury Manor here I come!'

Dusk was falling when at last Jenny came to the wrought-iron gates of

Embury Park. Her heart lifted as it always did when she saw glowing in the distance the beautiful red brick façade of the Tudor mansion. Up the long drive, flanked by ancient oaks, she drove and swept round the gravelled curve before the house into the private car-park.

Then she stood for a minute in front of the beautiful mansion. Above the imposing gate-house were carved the royal arms of England and the words 'DOM REX HENRICUS OCT'. The main building stretched to left and right of the portico with turrets at either end. The length of the façade was set with graceful Tudor windows, sparkling with diamond panes. Above rose a cluster of high twisted chimneys. Doves cooed in the eaves and all was peaceful.

It seemed to Jenny that the house slept, dreaming of the far off days when, to the blare of trumpets, Henry VIII and his enormous retinue had clattered through the gate-house into the courtyard beyond, filling it with exuberant life.

Following the steps of the royal charger, Jenny went through into the paved courtyard. The domestic buildings which once had surrounded it, had been demolished and replaced by a wall clothed with roses and clematis. Beyond, through an archway, lay the formal gardens, lovingly tended and now bright with summer flowers. In the far corner of the wall, entwined with honeysuckle, nestled a little cottage which once had housed, and later hidden, a priest.

Jenny turned to the west turret where her uncle had his quarters and with a thrill of daring pushed open the oaken door marked 'PRIVATE. NO ENTRY'. She had arrived.

'Is that you, Jenny?' called her aunt's voice. 'Come in darling!'

Jenny obeyed and found her aunt sitting in her elegant drawing-room, enthroned on a *chaise-longue* with her plastered leg stretched out before her.

'Oh, I am pleased to see you, darling!' she gushed, holding out her arms in an enveloping gesture. 'Come and kiss me. It's so good of you to come to my rescue at such short notice. I just couldn't get anyone else suitable. Sit down here beside me, sweetheart. Phyllis and Jean do their best but they really are getting past it and we're expecting coach-loads of American tourists.'

'I'm glad you didn't find anyone else,' smiled Jenny. 'You know how much I love Embury.'

'You are a sweetie! Henry, isn't she a sweetie?' demanded Aunt Sarah, turning to her husband who stood by with a somewhat cowed expression.

'Yes of course she is. Thank you Jenny,' he said, kissing her cheek.

'Well give the poor girl a drink,' commanded his wife. 'She's had a long journey.'

'Certainly dear,' he answered, turning to the drinks trolley. 'What would you like Jenny, sherry?'

'Oh, something long and cool. I am rather thirsty. Orangeade would be fine.'

Jenny sat down with her orangeade and, as she sipped it, retailed her mother's messages.

'However did you manage to fall?' she asked, when that duty had been accomplished.

Aunt Sarah shuddered delicately.

'I'd rather not talk about it. It makes me feel so silly,' she said.

'She wasn't looking where she was going,' said her husband.

'Nonsense, it was sheer accident!' snapped Sarah. 'Show Jenny up to her room and stop talking rubbish.'

'That's all right. I can find my own way,' said Jenny.

'Where have you put me?'

'The turret room. I know that's your favourite.'

'Oh yes! Thanks Aunt. I love the view over the countryside. When I was a child I used to pretend to be a beleaguered princess.'

'You were a funny little thing in those days.'

'I still am.'

'Imaginative,' put in Uncle Henry.

'I sincerely hope not,' said Aunt Sarah. 'Too much imagination is not good for a girl. Come on Henry, take Jenny's case up to her room and make yourself useful.'

Henry obediently picked up Jenny's case and she followed him up the winding stone staircase to the turret room.

'Thanks Uncle, you're a gem,' said Jenny as he put her case down on the bed.

'So are you,' he smiled.

'That makes two of us!' laughed Jenny and kissed him lightly to show her sympathy for his hen-pecked state.

'I'll take you round the house tomorrow,' he told her, swelling visibly, 'and show you the renovations I've been making. I'm quite proud of them.'

'So you should be,' said Jenny. 'I'll

look forward to seeing them.'

The two smiled at one another in friendly understanding.

'Dinner will be served at eight,' he announced assuming a pompous tone. 'We keep up our morale here despite all accidents.'

When he had gone Jenny stood looking out of the window at the well-remembered view. Across the courtyard a light was glimmering in the window of the Priest's House.

'One of Lord Mountfields' friends must be staying there,' she thought and turned away to unpack her case.

2

Jenny woke early the next morning, feeling delighted to find herself at Embury. She rolled out of bed and ran across the sloping floor to her turret window. She leaned far out breathing in the fresh morning air and the scent of a myriad flowers. Thin mist lay over the gardens and fields beyond, promising a hot day.

She dressed quickly, donning her favourite blue sundress and her white sandals in honour of Henry VIII, whose mighty presence still haunted the mansion. She hurried over her breakfast, so eager was she to explore again the gardens which had fascinated her as a child.

'I'll be ready to show you round at eleven o'clock,' said her uncle, as she turned to the door. 'I'll meet you in the gate-house and take you through the route we've mapped out for the visitors.'

'I'll be there,' promised Jenny and ran out into the sunshine. She wandered happily for a long time through the formal gardens, savouring each unexpected new vista revealed by every turn of the path. There were statues and terracotta urns to be greeted and a sundial which she checked by her watch to make sure the sun was doing its duty.

Along the pleached alley where once Elizabeth I had walked with one highly favoured swain or another, Jenny strolled and into the fountain court. Here a beautiful serpent coiled round and round with water continually gushing from its jaws. Peering through the rainbow lit by the spray, she saw in the far corner an artist seated on a rickety stool before his easel. He was a young man in paint-spattered jeans, the sleeves of his white shirt rolled up on his sunburnt arms. On his head was perched a battered straw hat shielding his eyes from the sun. So intent was he

on his work that he did not notice her
intrusion. The splashing of the fountain
drowned the noise of her footsteps as
she trod lightly up behind him, and
peered over his shoulder at his picture.
She saw a sunlit corner of the rose
garden with the ancient turrets of the
mansion rising above it.

'That's really quite good,' she
announced.

He stuck his paint brush in his
mouth and turned and saw a pretty girl
in a blue sundress, and liked what he
saw.

'What do you mean, quite good?' he
enquired, removing the brush from his
mouth. 'You're damning me with faint
praise.'

Jenny flushed.

'I'm sorry,' she said. 'I'm no critic, I
— I just meant that I liked it.'

'I'll forgive you if you tell me where
you've sprung from. We're not open for
visitors today.'

'I know. I'm here to help my aunt
with the visitors. She's broken her leg.

Now you can tell me what you're doing here.'

'That's easy. I'm boiling the pot.'

'You've chosen a lovely place to boil it.'

'Superb. When my agent came up with this assignment I snapped it up like a goldfish with a juicy fly. I'm not keen on starving in a garret, even if garrets were obtainable these days. I'm painting these little pot-boilers for sale in the shop. They'll be priceless one day.'

'You're sure of that?'

'Completely.'

'Then I'd better buy one before I go home.'

'I'll give you one if you'll do something for me.'

'What's that?'

'Pose for me.'

Jenny stepped back alarmed. A vision of a voluptuous female wantoning on a settee dressed in nothing but a black velvet neck-band rose to her inward eye.

'No!' she said sharply. 'Certainly not.'

Her reaction seemed to amuse him.

'Fully clothed of course and in the garden in full view of the public,' he said.

Jenny flushed, feeling a complete fool for having misunderstood.

'Not that you wouldn't look charming in a black velvet neck-band,' he grinned, seeming to read her thoughts.

'You can forget that, or I shan't even consider posing for you,' snapped Jenny.

He sobered at once.

'Coffee-time,' he said. 'Would you care to join me?'

'That depends on where you're serving it.'

'In the Priest's House of course. I'm living there until September.'

Jenny fell for the temptation.

'Well, I would like to see inside the Priest's House,' she said. 'It's always been tenanted when I've been here before.'

'I'll be delighted to show you round,' he said, getting to his feet. 'Follow me.'

Jenny obeyed, anxious to show that

she was not the foolish little provincial miss her embarrassment portrayed.

He flung open the door of the cottage with a wide gesture of hospitality. 'Come in,' he said, and ushered her in to a delightful little Elizabethan room, with whitewashed walls and a crooked ceiling supported by a large oak beam. At least it would have been delightful had it not been in a state of utter chaos. Clothes, paint, brushes, canvases, oily rags and dirty crockery were scattered around, inextricably mixed.

Jenny halted on the threshold.

'Oh good grief!' she exclaimed.

'What's wrong?' he enquired innocently.

'How can you work in such an appalling mess?'

'Mess? There's no mess. I know where everything is down to the last blob of paint.'

'But it's wicked to spoil such a beautiful Tudor room.'

'Rubbish. I bet it wasn't all tarted up when a priest lived here. He'd be too busy praying or plotting to murder the Queen to bother with housework. Come on in and I'll get the coffee.'

He picked up a mug from the floor and another from the window sill, and carried them into the kitchen.

'I'll put the kettle on,' he said.

'You'll have to let me wash those mugs first,' said Jenny, following him.

'If you must. But it seems a waste of time when we're just going to put more coffee in them.'

Jenny did not deign to reply, but took the mugs out of his hands and rinsed them under the tap.

She was relieved to find that the kitchen was clean and neat. The saucepans on the shelf above the cooker were shining, and the cooker itself was spotless. Apart from a heap of corned-beef tins in a bucket in a corner and a dish of tomatoes on the draining board, all was spick and span.

'Well at least you're a careful cook,' she said.

'I'm not a cook at all. I'm too busy. I

live on corned-beef and tomatoes.'

Jenny shuddered.

'What you need is a wife,' she said.

'Oh no, I don't! Heaven forbid!' he retorted. 'I value my freedom.'

'So you're beyond redemption.'

'Utterly.'

'Then I won't bother to find you a suitable girl. Where's the coffee?'

'In the tin marked 'sugar'.'

'It would be. Where's the sugar? In the tin marked 'linseed oil'?'

'Of course not! What a daft suggestion. It's in the tin marked 'arsenic'. Where else?'

Jenny laughed, warming to this impossible man.

'Kettle's boiling,' she said.

When the coffee was made Jenny returned to the living-room and stood in the midst of the chaos itching to clear it up.

'We'll sit outside,' said the artist, 'I can see a malicious glint in your eye.'

He carried the mugs out into the garden and they sat together on a bench

24

against the cottage wall.

'I'm Alan Freeman, at your service,' he said, holding out a paint-stained hand.

'Jenny Collins,' replied Jenny, shaking it solemnly.

'Good, now we're properly introduced, we can be friends,' said Alan.

They sat for a minute in companionable silence. It was very peaceful there in the garden with only the sound of a light wind stirring the trees and doves cooing from the medieval dovecot. The turrets and twisted chimneys of Embury Court rose romantically above the trees.

'When I'm rich and famous I'm going to have a house like Embury,' said Alan. 'Not quite so large of course, but the same style.'

'It sounds wonderful. Will you ask me to come and stay?'

'Of course, you shall have an open invitation.'

'Will that include my husband and children?'

He choked and spilt his coffee down his shirt.

'Are you really married?' he asked.

Jenny laughed. 'Not yet, but I intend to be soon,' she said.

'Have you chosen your intended?'

'No, he hasn't appeared yet, but he will.'

'So you've got it all mapped out. Have you fixed where you're going to live to nurture your brood?'

'In a semi-detached in Purley, I suppose. We shan't be able to afford anything grander.'

'You'll hate that.'

'I shall have to put up with it, shan't I? Unless I meet a millionaire.'

He raised his coffee mug high. 'To Jenny's millionaire,' he said, 'may he soon put in an appearance.'

'Hear! Hear! I'll drink to that,' said Jenny and clinked mugs with him.

'You're giving me ideas above my station,' she said. 'I'm only a very ordinary primary-school teacher.'

'Rubbish! Ordinary you are not,' he said decisively. 'I'm planning an exhibition at the Exton Gallery in the autumn.

Your portrait will be the central attraction.'

'I haven't said I'll pose for you yet.'

'I want to start early tomorrow to get the best light,' he continued, ignoring her protest. 'I want you just as you are now, in that blue frock and white sandals. Be here at nine o'clock sharp.'

Jenny stood up and handed him her empty coffee cup.

'I might, on the other hand I might not,' she said. 'I've got to go now. Thanks for the coffee.'

She turned and ran down the alley towards the house.

'Nine o'clock sharp!' he called after her retreating back.

He watched her supple young figure with appreciation.

'Truly Lady Luck is on my side at last,' he congratulated himself.

Jenny's uncle was waiting for her in the gate-house as arranged.

'You look flushed,' he said. 'What have you been up to?'

'Talking to the artist who's staying in

the Priest's House. He gave me coffee.'

'Alan Freeman, yes, he's a decent chap. He gave me a lot of useful advice with the renovations.'

'Is he really as talented as he thinks he is?'

'Well, I believe he's well thought of in artistic circles. The water-colours he's painted for the shop are very popular. They're pretty pricey but the visitors snap them up.'

'He says they'll fetch millions when he's famous.'

Uncle Henry laughed tolerantly.

'Oh well, it's the privilege of youth to dream, I suppose,' he said. 'Now come along, my dear, we'll go through the rooms open to the public, just to remind you of the questions you're likely to be asked.'

'I know the questions. It's the answers I need to learn,' said Jenny.

Their tour proceeded as planned through the most ancient part of the mansion. They went first through the Great Hall with its long trestle-table, fashioned out of the trunk of a single oak tree, then they climbed up the winding stair into the Long Gallery where the Tudor portraits, the pride of Embury Court were hung.

At the far end of the gallery, Henry VIII stood four-square, glaring at all intruders as though longing to send them to the Tower. To his left were ranged his six wives, all solemn and wary-eyed, afraid to utter a word lest it be the wrong one. On his right was his unhappy elder daughter, Mary, her thin lips closed against all emotion after a lifetime of suffering and persecution. Facing her father, as haughty as he, hung Elizabeth I in all her finery, gazing down on her people, demanding adoration.

Jenny loved these portraits. They were a history-book in themselves. She walked along the gallery slowly, greeting them like old friends. Beyond the gallery was a small apartment filled with an enormous four-poster bed. Because of the bed, this was known as

Henry VIII's bedchamber.

From this miraculously well-preserved sixteenth-century section of the mansion, the visitor stepped into the eighteenth-century, a world of greater comfort and luxury. A stone passage led to the rooms which later Mountfields, sparing no expense, had transformed for their own use. The jewel of this suite was known as the Pink Drawing-room because of its elaborate rose-patterned wallpaper and Persian carpet. Here were housed the treasures which generations of Mountfields had brought back from the Grand Tours of their youth. Venetian glass, French silver and china from the Low Countries were set out for the delight of the visitor.

'You've re-hung the pictures, haven't you Uncle Henry?' asked Jenny. 'They're in a much better light.'

'Yes,' said her uncle, 'Alan Freeman advised me on that. It's certainly an improvement.'

Jenny turned next to greet two old favourites, the silver teapot from which the Queen Mother had once poured tea, and the black Egyptian cat, carved out of ebony. He sat atop a cabinet, very straight and proud, rivalling the Tudors in arrogance, for he knew he was a god.

'But where are the Donalettos?' asked Jenny, suddenly realizing there were treasures missing. 'Surely Lord Mountfields hasn't sold them!'

'Not yet, but they may have to go soon,' said her uncle. 'Cash is pretty tight and the house is badly in need of repair. But they're still here. We've re-sited them in the writing-room!'

He conducted Jenny into a little room opening off the drawing-room. This was known as the writing-room and was a cosy sanctuary where the Lords of Embury could escape from the ladies and pretend to be busy. It housed a fine rosewood escritoire on which lay a tooled leather writing-case, bearing the Mountfields' arms, and a pewter inkwell and quill pens. On each of the four walls of this sanctum was now hung a priceless heirloom, paintings of old Venice by the Italian master Donaletto.

'Oh yes!' cried Jenny when she saw them. 'This is the perfect place for them.'

'Alan Freeman's judgement again, not mine,' smiled her uncle.

Beyond the Pink Drawing-room and its annexe was a graceful oak staircase which led to bedrooms furnished in elaborate eighteenth-century style. On its panelled walls were hung portraits of the Mountfields' ancestors. Jenny paused as usual before the picture of a smiling young bride which her aunt and uncle declared was like herself. Jenny smiled back at her, feeling flattered at the supposed resemblance.

When the tour was over Jenny felt she had come home to a kingdom where she had reigned in her imagination since her childhood.

'You won't feel nervous about conducting the American visitors tomorrow, will you?' asked her uncle. 'I could put off my trip to London if you like.'

'No, of course I shan't be nervous,' laughed Jenny. 'You forget I'm used to haranguing a crowd!'

★　★　★

Over supper that evening, Jenny's aunt voiced the same worry.

'Now are you sure you can manage?' she asked. 'There'll be Japanese visitors as well, you know. I can get Mabel in to help if you like?'

'There's no need, she'd only be a distraction.'

'I feel so helpless with this leg,' complained her aunt.

'Stop worrying, do. I'm used to controlling a howling mob of six-year-olds. A coach-load of visitors will be a doddle.'

'Don't let anyone touch the Tudor portraits, and keep them off the carpet in the Pink Drawing-room. Make them stay on the drugget, and above all don't let anyone so much as breathe on the china, it's already showing hair-cracks.'

'Stop worrying!' repeated Jenny. 'I met the artist who's living in the Priest's House,' she added, hoping to change the subject.

Aunt Sarah looked disdainful.

'A very raffish young man,' she said.

'Why do you say that dear?' asked Uncle Henry. 'I found him most helpful.'

'It's those filthy jeans he wears, he makes me shudder.'

'But they are his working clothes, dear. You can't expect him to paint in a business suit.'

'Of course not Henry, I'm not so silly as you seem to think. But he might at least wash them occasionally. I do hope he's keeping the cottage clean. It took Doris two days to clean it after the last tenant.'

'It's absolutely immaculate,' lied Jenny. 'You'd be surprised!'

'I certainly should. I'll believe it when I see it.'

'I liked him!' said Jenny stoutly. 'He asked me to pose for him.'

'What impertinence! You refused of course?'

'I said I'd think about it.'

Even Uncle Henry looked doubtful at this.

'I don't really think it would be wise,' he warned.

Jenny laughed.

'Fully clothed, and in the garden,' she said. 'I'll be quite safe.'

'I dare say,' sniffed Aunt Sarah, 'but I don't think you should do it. I'm sure your mother would say the same, and I'm in her place while you're with me.'

'Aunt Sarah!' cried Jenny. 'I'm twenty-two! I don't need mothering!'

'I'm not so sure of that, either,' said Aunt Sarah.

If she had known Jenny better she would have realized that this was not the way to deter her headstrong niece.

Thus, the next morning Jenny gave Alan five minutes to get worried and then presented herself at the Priest's House, in her blue dress and white sandals.

'You're late,' he said.

'You're lucky I came at all. My aunt did her best to dissuade me.'

'Why? What has she got against me?'

'She thinks you're raffish.'

'Raffish! I've been called a lot of things in my time but never raffish. What does it mean?'

'Dissolute and disreputable.'

'Well you can tell your aunt that I'd love to oblige her but I haven't got time to be either. Let's get a move on. We've wasted ten minutes already.'

He took her arm and propelled her into the herb garden where he had set up his easel before a nude statue of Venus.

'I want you standing by her,' he said. 'Put your hand on her arm and pretend you're talking to her.'

Jenny obeyed and he sketched in silence for a while.

'You're too stiff,' he said at last. 'Pretend you're talking to her.'

'I am.'

36

'What are you saying?'

'I'm advising her to go to Oxfam and buy some clothes.'

'And what does she say to that?'

'She says I'm jealous because the Earl of Essex admired her figure. She says Queen Elizabeth was so jealous she ordered her to be draped in a white sheet.'

'She's lying, of course.'

At that Jenny threw her head back and laughed aloud.

'Beautiful!' said Alan. 'Hold it!'

He worked on industriously with a smile of pleasure on his face. After what seemed an hour to Jenny, he sat back and sighed happily.

'This is going to be my masterpiece,' he said. 'I feel it in my bones.'

'It's my bones that are suffering,' protested Jenny. 'I ache all over.'

'Relax and rest,' he told her. 'I've made a good start. I can see it all in my head. It's now only a matter of getting it on to the canvas.'

Jenny collapsed with a sigh of relief

and sat down with her back against the statue.

'Then you won't need me any more,' she said.

'Oh yes I shall,' he replied. 'I shall want you tomorrow and the next day.'

'I'll have to think about it.'

'You won't back out now. You're the type to see a project through once you've started it.'

'So you think you know me.'

'I can read you like a book. You agreed to pose for me because you thought a raffish artist would be a bit of a thrill.'

'Wrong! I came because my uncle said you were harmless.'

'Harmless! What an insult! I'd rather be raffish than harmless. It sounds like the village idiot. ' 'He's not right in the head, my dear, but harmless',' he mimicked, putting on a falsetto voice.

'What do you think you deserve as an epitaph?'

'He was perfect in every way. We shall

not look upon his like again.'

'Good job too! I'll leave you now to polish your halo. I've got to conduct a tour this afternoon.'

'And you're nervous.'

'Not in the least! That's further proof that you don't know me.'

'Aha! So you're hoping to find your millionaire amongst the tourists.'

'Now I know you're an idiot!'

'But raffish with it!'

They were still laughing when there appeared round the corner of the herb garden an invalid-chair wheeled by a stalwart gardener. In it sat Aunt Sarah like Boadicea in her chariot.

Alan stood up politely.

'Good morning Mrs Dixon,' he said.

'Good morning Mr Freeman,' she answered icily. 'I'm afraid I must take your model away. She is here as my helper you know, and I need her back at the house.'

'That's quite all right, Mrs Dixon,' replied Alan smoothly, 'I've finished for this morning.'

'Come along Jenny please,' snapped Aunt Sarah.

Jenny scrambled to her feet and turned to give Venus a farewell pat on her bottom.

'Tomorrow, nine a.m. and don't be late,' Alan whispered.

'Perhaps,' replied Jenny.

The project was all the more interesting now it had become a conspiracy, but it would be good for him to keep wondering.

3

Despite her bold words Jenny was in fact very nervous at the approach of her first stint as a guide. Managing a class of infants was very different from coping with a party of adults many of whom might be more knowledgeable than herself. However she approached the ordeal with her usual determination. Head held high, she walked firmly into the gate-house and greeted the waiting crowd with a bright smile.

'Good afternoon, ladies and gentlemen,' she said. 'Welcome to Embury Court. I am your guide this afternoon.'

As the visitors murmured their appreciation she looked them over, hoping, though she would not admit it, to find her millionaire among them. They were, of course, the usual assorted crowd of tourists. All doubtless delightful in their own way, but not for her.

Taking herself firmly in hand, Jenny commenced her lecture.

'You are now standing in the Tudor gate-house,' she announced. 'It has hardly changed since Henry VIII himself rode through on one of his frequent visits.'

'How long ago was that?' asked an eager voice.

'Oh, getting on for five hundred years.'

There was a general gasp of astonishment at such great antiquity.

'Was Anne Boleyn with him?' enquired a romantic lady.

'Not this time, she'd already met her come-uppance,' explained Jenny. 'He had with him another charmer, Catherine Howard. Actually she was a far more wanton type than poor old Anne. I don't know why she doesn't get so much publicity. You'll see her portrait when we come to the Long Gallery and you can judge for yourselves.'

The visitors' eyes goggled at the

thought of so much wickedness and Jenny gained confidence.

She led her audience into the Great Hall.

'This is where all the feasting and carousing went on,' she said, 'and where Henry VIII's jester cracked his jokes. He was the Bob Monkhouse of the Court.'

A laugh went up at this sally and Jenny's spirits rose. She was going over well. She began to enjoy herself.

She conveyed the visitors smoothly through the Long Gallery and up the stairs leading to the later part of the house, answering all their questions with an air of profound learning. They laughed at the mildly scandalous tales of the antics of the Mountfields' ancestors whose portraits lined the walls of the staircase, and gasped at the age and beauty of the treasures on show in the Pink Drawing-room.

As they toured the bedrooms, she noticed that a tall, young man had joined the party. She could not help her heart fluttering at the sight of him for he was disturbingly handsome and carried himself in a supremely self-confident manner. The newcomer fixed his eyes upon her and appeared to be enthralled by her words of wisdom.

When the tour was over Jenny conducted her flock to the exit and pointed out the tea-room and souvenir shop across the courtyard. There was a chorus of thanks and appreciation of her skill, and then they all trooped out obediently — all except the handsome stranger. He had not followed the others and Jenny had to go back to look for him. She found him standing in the Pink Drawing-room, awaiting her coming.

'I enjoyed that,' he said, looking down upon her admiringly. 'I never knew the old place was so interesting.'

'Thank you,' said Jenny, trying to look modest. 'I'm afraid the tour is over now. You'll find some delightful souvenirs in the shop if you follow the others.'

He did not obey her command, but swung his long legs over the rope separating the tourists from the treasures, walked boldly over the Persian carpet and picked up the Queen Mother's silver teapot.

'I can just imagine Queen Anne pouring 'tay' from this,' he said.

'It's Georgian,' snapped Jenny. 'Put it down please.'

He laughed, flourishing the teapot carelessly.

'I don't suppose those alcoholic old Georges drank much tea,' he said.

Jenny flushed angrily. 'Come off the carpet at once,' she snapped. 'These treasures are not your playthings.'

'Oh, but they are,' he replied. 'I'm Gerald Mountfields. These things are all mine, or will be when my father joins the ancestors.'

'They are not yours and never will be,' barked Jenny furiously. 'They belong to the nation. Your father holds them in trust. Put the teapot down and come off the carpet at once.'

He returned to her side, grinning.

'You look delightful when you're angry,' he said.

Jenny boiled with rage. He was so unfairly attractive. She hated him.

'Now go!' she ordered. 'I have to lock up.'

'I'll go if you'll join me for tea,' he said. 'You must be thirsty after so much talking.'

'Certainly not,' snapped Jenny. 'This way please.'

'Oh dear, I have got off on the wrong footing,' he laughed. 'I'd better go out and come in again.'

'Go out, but don't bother to come in again. Goodbye!'

She slammed the door shut behind him and turned the key with a savage twist. His swaggering virility disturbed her. She could have killed him.

'Until we meet again,' he said, bowing gracefully and strolled away towards Lord Mountfields' private apartments.

'What a sickening, slimy toad!'

muttered Jenny. 'Dear God, I thought I was never going to get rid of him.'

She took several deep breaths to calm herself before she went to report progress to her aunt.

She found her sitting behind her own silver teapot, waiting anxiously to hear Jenny's report.

'Well, how did you get on?' she asked at once.

'Fine!' said Jenny, flopping into a chair.

'You look flushed,' said her aunt. 'Did you have any trouble?'

'None at all,' lied Jenny. 'Everyone was most appreciative.'

'Thank you darling,' said her aunt with a sigh of relief. 'I knew you wouldn't let me down. Now sit back and enjoy your tea. I expect you're thirsty.'

'Gasping!' said Jenny, managing a smile.

She leant back and echoed her aunt's sigh of relief. Alas her peace did not last long. She was just sipping her second cup of tea when the housekeeper opened the door and announced in an awed voice, 'The Honourable Gerald Mountfields, madam.'

Jenny choked with dismay, but her aunt flushed with surprise and delight.

'How kind of you to call!' she gushed. 'Do excuse my not getting up, but I've broken my leg as you can see. So silly of me!'

'Oh please don't disturb yourself,' he answered, oozing *politesse*. 'May I sit here, next to your other visitor?' And he sat himself down on the sofa next to Jenny.

She shifted away from him as far as she could, but he affected not to notice.

'I don't think I know your guest. Please do introduce me,' he requested his hostess smoothly. 'We met at this afternoon's tour, but I didn't learn her name.'

'Oh dear! How remiss of me!' cried Aunt Sarah. 'My niece, Jenny Collins, she's here to help me with the tourists until I can walk again.'

'But of course!' he smiled. 'I might have guessed. Our guides are usually elderly and dowdy. I couldn't think where such a charmer had sprung from.'

Jenny glared at him ferociously but he was not in the least abashed.

'I'm feeling rather lonely at the moment,' he continued smoothly. 'I gather there's a hop at the village hall on Saturday. Would you take pity on me, Miss Collins, and allow me to escort you there?'

'No thank you,' snapped Jenny. 'I'm not all that fond of village hops.'

'Nonsense, Jenny! You'd enjoy it,' exclaimed her aunt. 'You haven't any young friends here either. Do go.'

'That's not the point, Aunt Sarah,' replied her obdurate niece, 'I came here to help you, not to enjoy myself.'

Gerry uncurled his long length from the sofa and stood up.

'Perhaps some other time,' he said with a charming smile, 'when your aunt is out of plaster.'

'Yes, of course she will!' cried Sarah. 'I shall soon be walking about as good as new. I wonder — since you're lonely — whether you'd care to dine with us one evening.'

'I should be delighted.'

'Then shall we say next Thursday?'

'That would suit me admirably,' he purred. 'Well, until next Thursday then.'

As soon as the door closed behind their distinguished visitor, Jenny turned on her aunt.

'How could you?' she demanded.

'Why, what have I done wrong?'

'Toadying round that arrogant monster! He's laughing at you.'

'Rubbish! He accepted my invitation fast enough. As a matter of fact I think he's rather attracted to you.'

'Well he can forget that. I'm not one of his bimbos.'

'I really don't understand you Jenny. Most girls would give their eye-teeth for an invitation from him.'

'They can keep him. I'm going out to

get some fresh air.'

Jenny stormed out, her stomach churning. She walked round the deer park, trying to calm herself. She knew she had overreacted to Gerry's invitation. The cheek of the monster! How she wished he was not so damned attractive.

The next morning, Jenny dressed quickly and ran out into the soft sunshine. She was determined not to let the insufferable Gerald ruin her stay at Embury. Rejoicing in the fresh morning air and the happy song of the birds, she walked through the gardens to the lake. She stood on the bank gazing out across the still water. Willow trees leant towards it, trailing their branches in the water and throwing dark green mysterious shadows across its surface. Beyond the shadows where the sun sparkled, ducks bobbed and paddled.

Jenny had always loved the lake. As a child she had woven many a story around its alluring depths. Shaking herself free of memories, she began to walk along the path which skirted the banks. As she walked, a man came towards her through the trees. It was Gerald. Her heart sank. There was no way of avoiding him save by undignified flight. She went forward firmly.

'Good morning, Miss Collins,' he greeted her with a charming smile. 'I see you admire my lake.'

'It's not your lake!'

'Oh yes it is. It's always been mine. I had many a wild adventure on it when I was a boy.'

Jenny softened. Perhaps he was not so bad after all, she thought.

'I used to play here too when I was a child,' she said.

'I was at school then, I expect. Cruelly banished from home. Aren't you sorry for that poor boy, Miss Collins?'

'For heaven's sake stop calling me Miss Collins. You sound like a Victorian novel.'

'May I call you Jenny, then?'

'It's my name.'

'Mine's Gerry. What about making friends?'

'I suppose we'd better since we're not going to be able to avoid each other,' said Jenny reluctantly.

'Good. Would you like to come for a row on the lake? I've got the key to the boat-house.'

Jenny looked out across the gently rippling green water. It was very alluring. She fell to the tempter's art.

'Thanks,' she said. 'Yes I'd like to.'

Gerry took her arm in companionable fashion and led her to the little wooden shed at the head of the lake. He pushed out the rowing-boat and helped her climb in.

Jenny sat in the stern and trailed her hand in the water as he rowed with strong strokes into the middle of the lake.

'Enjoying yourself?' he enquired with a smile.

'I'm loving it,' she replied.

'Then we've no need to go ashore ever again.'

'We'll get hungry.'

'I'll catch a fish.'

Jenny laughed. No, Gerry was not at all bad when you got to know him. In fact he was rather nice.

When they reached the far side of the lake Jenny returned to reality with a harsh jerk. She glanced at her watch. It was nearly a quarter to ten! She had been floating in a beautiful dream for nearly an hour.

'Put me ashore quickly,' she told Gerry. 'I promised I'd join Alan Freeman at half-past nine.'

'That oaf? Whatever for?'

'He's painting my portrait, and he's not an oaf, he's very talented.'

'So he keeps saying. Well it won't hurt him to wait a bit longer.'

With a practised twist of the oars, Gerry turned the boat round and began to row out into the middle of the lake again.

'Oh come on, Gerry. Stop playing tricks. Put me ashore at once or I'll never come out with you again.'

'Ah! Now I've caught you. If I let you

land will you promise to come rowing with me again?'

'All right, provided you promise no more infantile tricks.'

'It's a deal. What about tomorrow?'

'That's a date. Now land-ho!'

Obediently Gerry grounded the boat on the shore and helped Jenny alight.

'See you tomorrow without fail,' he said.

Jenny stepped ashore thankfully. For one horrible moment she had thought she was trapped.

'Thanks for the ride,' she said and ran swiftly through the gardens to find Alan.

She found him sitting on the bench outside the Priest's House, clutching a mug of coffee and looking very sour.

'We said nine o'clock,' he growled.

'I'm sorry. I got delayed. But I'm here now. Let's begin.'

'It's too late, I've lost the best of the light.'

'Well cheer up. There's still tomorrow.'

'If the weather holds.'

'There's no sign of a break,' said Jenny, sitting down beside him on the bench. 'Now dry your eyes and get me a cup of coffee to show there's no ill-feeling.'

'But there is ill-feeling. Gallons of it.'

'Swallow it down like a man and get the coffee and I'll have two digestive biscuits with it.'

Alan managed a twisted smile and obeyed. Jenny's blue eyes were very appealing.

'What was it delayed you?' he asked when he returned.

'I went on the lake with Gerry Mountfields and forgot the time.'

'That rat! Is he around again?'

'Very much so. He's not all that bad when you get to know him.'

'I've no intention of getting to know him, ever.'

Jenny laughed. 'Men are such idiots,' she said. 'They think they're the most important creatures on earth.'

'So we are. At least my painting is the

most important project here. Gerald is just fooling around wasting his time. Why doesn't he get out a book and learn something?'

'He's on holiday!'

'Well I'm not. I'm working. I only need one more session with you, Jenny. Promise me you'll be here tomorrow at nine o'clock sharp.'

'All right I promise.'

'And you'll avoid the lures of that blighter, Gerald?'

'Oh, it's not Gerry that lures me. It's his boat.'

'Then resist the enchantment of the boat, and don't let me down again or I shall be deeply disappointed in you.'

'I wouldn't disappoint you for the world,' laughed Jenny. 'Now I'll leave you to simmer quietly. I've got a tour to conduct this afternoon.'

She ran off smiling. She had promised her company to two rival young men. She was enjoying herself.

'Where have you been?' asked Aunt

Sarah in the manner of aunts every-
where when Jenny appeared.

'I've been rowing on the lake with
Gerald Mountfields.'

Aunt Sarah's face softened and her
eyes lit up at the sound of her hero's
name.

'I'm so glad you've made friends with
him, dear,' she said. 'He's such a
charming young man. I can't think why
you were so stand-offish before.'

'He's far too pushy. He needs to be
kept in his place,' said Jenny. 'But I can
handle him.'

The afternoon tour went smoothly
and the tourists were most appreciative.
Jenny directed them to Alan's paintings,
which were much admired and to her
pleasure sold well.

'I think Gerald Mountfields seriously
admires Jenny,' said her aunt to her
husband later.

'She's a very attractive girl,' agreed
Henry. 'But whether he's serious is
another matter, you'd better warn her
to beware.'

'Don't be so old-fashioned!' exclaimed Sarah. 'This is the nineties. Girls are different from what they were in your young days.'

'Girls may be different but young men are still the same, I'll be bound.'

'Nonsense. Gerald is very charming and completely trustworthy, I'm sure.'

'The charming ones are always the worst,' said Henry dourly. 'I shall keep a sharp eye on him.'

'Now Henry, you've not to interfere or you'll spoil everything. Gerald is the most eligible bachelor in England.'

'That does not reassure me.'

'Well I'm delighted with this development, but you're hopeless. It's useless talking to you,' snapped Aunt Sarah. And that ended the conversation.

Gerald, however, was not delighted when, on the morrow, Jenny told him she was breaking her promise.

'I'm sorry,' she said, 'but this is work.'

'Whose work, yours or Alan's?'

'Both of course. I'm helping him!'

'He needs all the help he can get, I

shouldn't be surprised. But I don't see why I should be sacrificed to his footling demands.'

'Stop moaning and I'll come with you tomorrow.'

'Right, that's a date. I'm coming to dinner with you tomorrow. We'll go for a row afterwards. The moon will be full. You'll love it.'

'If you say so.'

'I do. Follow me, my child, and you won't go far wrong.'

'Are you sure you want to come to dinner? It will be horribly boring.'

'No it won't. I'm looking forward to it.'

'Very well then. On your head be it.'

'That's arranged then.'

'Yes. See you this evening.'

She left Gerry smiling gleefully and ran off to keep her promise to Alan.

'Who'd have believed that dear old Embury could be so exciting?' she laughed to herself as she ran.

4

Alan was waiting at the rendezvous, easel and paints at the ready.

'Good, you're here. Let's get on,' was his terse greeting.

The session proceeded smoothly at first and all seemed to be going well, when a dark shadow fell across Alan's easel. Gerald Mountfields had come up behind him and was peering over his shoulder.

'That's rather good,' he said. 'I'll buy it from you.'

'It's not for sale.'

'I'll pay a good price.'

'It's not for sale at any price. Now get out of the light. I'm busy.'

Gerald stepped aside and smiled across at Jenny.

'Don't let this bad-tempered blighter bully you,' he said.

'Go away, Gerry,' said Jenny, 'and

don't be a pest or I shan't come out with you tomorrow.'

'Oh yes you will. I'll see to that. Your aunt's on my side.'

'Buzz off!'

Gerald grinned an all-conquering grin.

'Do I gather that you want to be rid of me?' he asked. 'How odd! See you tomorrow evening. Meanwhile I'll conquer my impatience by going for a gallop on Dobbin.'

'I hope you fall off and break your neck,' muttered Alan as the intruder departed.

'Calm down, do!' said Jenny. 'And get on with your work.'

'But surely you're not going out with that lecher!'

'He's harmless enough if you keep him under control. I'm only going for a moonlit row on the lake. You'll hear me if I scream and you can come and rescue me.'

'I'll do just that,' promised Alan. 'I know the type. Wolves in human shape.'

'Why do you dislike him so much?' asked Jenny innocently.

'I hate the idle rich. They batten on society. Why doesn't he do something constructive?'

'He's reading for the bar.'

'Then he'd better go away and do just that, and stop plaguing you.'

'He's not plaguing me. I quite like him,' said Jenny, deliberately provocative.

However, as Thursday evening drew nearer she began to regret her rash promise to Gerry. She decided it was better to be safe than sorry. She would stay safely at her aunt's side and pretend to have forgotten all about the moonlight. She was not to escape so easily, for Gerald was used to getting his own way.

The dinner was a success. Gerald was at his charming best. He admired Aunt Sarah's decor, ate with evident relish everything he was offered, discussed with Henry the renovations to the mansion and thanked him gracefully for all the work he had put in. Then he turned to Jenny and passed on Lord Mountfields' praise of her skill with the tourists.

'He's received many enthusiastic comments,' he smiled.

Finally he sipped his coffee slowly and showed no unmannerly haste to be gone.

When at last he rose he met with no opposition to his plan for a row in the moonlight. Aunt Sarah glowed with satisfaction, and Jenny felt perfectly safe with such a delightful companion. In this atmosphere of mutual gratification Uncle Henry could hardly object.

Jenny stepped out into the summer night boldly and took Gerry's arm. She had been an idiot to let Uncle Henry's old-fashioned ideas influence her. She could deal with a regiment of Gerry's.

The lake was indeed lovelier than ever in the moonlight. The full moon threw a magical path of silver light across the water and there was no sound save mysterious rustlings in the reeds by the lake's edge. All nature seemed to hold its breath as though waiting for the ghosts of the past centuries at Embury to walk and laugh and make love again.

Jenny was enchanted. 'It's like a scene from a fairy story,' she said.

Gerry put his arm round her waist and pulled her nearer.

'Am I the prince?' he asked.

'Oh no! The story's only just begun. You're the kindly old bear who helps the princess in her search for the prince.'

'But the bear always sheds his bear-skin at the end and reveals himself to be the prince.'

'Maybe, but there are all sorts of ordeals and dangers for him to go through first.'

'I'm ready for them all. Come on let's sample the ordeal by water.'

Gerry led her to the boat which bobbed invitingly at the little jetty and carefully helped her in. Jenny allowed herself to be helped, although she could have leapt in quite safely. It was pleasant to be treated like a precious but fragile princess.

The boat drifted gently down the moon's silver pathway, only the soft splash of the oars breaking the silence of the night. Somewhere an owl hooted and a captured mouse squeaked. The spell was shattered.

Gerry rested on the oars and let the boat drift. He had never been far from reality though it pleased him that Jenny should dream in a fairy-tale world. He looked across at her and smiled.

'I never thought I should meet a girl like you,' he said. 'All the girls at Cambridge were either plain and earnest with long black skirts and greasy hair, or they were frivolous and over-made-up and only out for a good time. You're the first girl I've ever met who's both beautiful and serious.'

'But not very clever, or I wouldn't be sitting in this boat in the moonlight with you.'

He laughed.

'Are you afraid my intentions are not

honourable, Miss Collins?' he asked.

Jenny flushed, realizing he was laughing at her lack of sophistication. He stood up, meaning to come and sit beside her. The boat rocked. Angry that he thought her such easy game, Jenny pushed him. He fell with a splash into the water. Quickly she seized an oar and propelled herself back to the shore.

'Help!' Gerry shouted. 'Help! I can't swim!'

'Then you'll have to drown!' Jenny shouted back, and feeling the ground beneath the boat's keel, leapt ashore, and ran through the trees. With a practised crawl Gerry swam across the lake, clambered ashore and ran after her. Pounding through the bushes with his long legs, he soon caught up with her and seized her in his arms.

'You little fiend!' he gasped, and kissed her firmly on the lips. Jenny's body yielded to his, but only for a second. Realizing her predicament she twisted and turned to free herself.

'Let me go,' she begged. 'You're

making me wet.'

'Why not? You've made me wet,' he laughed. 'Stop struggling. I've passed the ordeal by water.'

'Oh no you haven't. You shouted for help. That's not heroic. Let me go at once!'

She put her hands against his shoulders and pushed with all her might. For a moment his grip slackened and she wrenched herself out of his grasp and ran off towards the house. He did not pursue her, but stood in the darkness smiling to himself. He had felt her body yield and was sure that his victory was not far off.

Jenny found her Uncle Henry anxiously waiting up for her. She put her head round the sitting-room door and smiled at him.

'Here I am, safe and sound,' she called. 'You are an old dinosaur!'

'Come in and kiss me good-night,' he replied.

She did so reluctantly, for she did not want him to see her wet frock, but she could not avoid his concerned enquiries.

'Why are you so wet?' he asked at once.

Jenny laughed carelessly.

'It's nothing. I got splashed,' she answered. 'Goodnight Uncle.'

She kissed him lightly on the top of his head and escaped up to her room. Her heart was thumping and her head in a whirl. She had enjoyed it in Gerry's arms too much for comfort. With a delicious thrill of fear, she wondered what his next ploy would be.

Gerry however, played his fish carefully. He did not approach her again for a few days, leaving her to wonder.

'Oh very well, please yourself,' Jenny told him inwardly when he did not appear. 'I'll go and see how Alan's getting on.'

She found him sitting at his easel in a corner of the garden, sketching the view through the rose arbour to the Tudor gateway in the ancient wall.

He smiled when he saw her approaching.

'So you've not forgotten me,' he said.

'How could I ever?'

'Only too easily I suspect. Have you come to see your portrait?'

'I'd like to if it's on show.'

He got up and took her hand.

'Come on then,' he said, drawing her with him. 'It's standing proudly in the place of honour. I'm very pleased with it actually.'

Jenny was delighted with the picture. All Alan's talent had gone into its making. The grey-green of the worn stone of the statue contrasted vividly with the warm flesh of the girl beside it.

'You've flattered me,' she said.

'Of course. That's my artistic skill.'

'Pig! You should have said that no paint could equal the real thing!'

'Oh no! It's me viewers are supposed to be admiring, not the model!'

'Hard luck! They obviously won't.'

'I suspect that you're right. But don't let's quarrel over it. I'm thinking of taking a break and going for a trip to the sea. Would you come with me?'

'Yes, I'd love to. A breath of sea air would be just what the doctor ordered.'

'What about tomorrow then? If you've not got a tour to conduct.'

'No, I'm free tomorrow. That's a date then,' agreed Jenny.

'Fine! I'll get my old jalopy tuned up. She does rattle a bit but she'll get us there.'

This time it was Aunt Sarah who objected when Jenny announced her plans at breakfast.

'Surely you're not going out with that raffish young man!' she exclaimed.

'Why not? He's good fun.'

'Fun! And Weymouth of all places in the middle of August! There won't be room to move on the beach.'

'We'll find a few inches where we can sit and eat our sandwiches.'

'I'll never understand you young people nowadays. You have all these lovely grounds and you want to go and pig it at Weymouth!'

71

'I'll appreciate it all the better when I come back,' laughed Jenny.

'Now Sarah, don't nag the poor girl,' interrupted Uncle Henry. 'She deserves a day off after all her hard work.'

Aunt Sarah subsided, muttering, 'That frightful young man and that awful car! I just don't understand you Jenny.'

'I'll tell you all about the horrors this evening,' said Jenny. 'Now I'm going to the kitchen to see about some corned-beef sandwiches.'

'Corned-beef sandwiches!' moaned Aunt Sarah.

'It'll do young Gerald Mountfields good to know he's got a rival,' soothed Uncle Henry.

Aunt Sarah brightened.

'Yes, that's true!' she exclaimed. 'Perhaps Jenny's not so stupid after all.'

'I keep telling you she knows what she's doing,' said Uncle Henry. 'At least I hope so.'

When that afternoon Gerry came to call to invite Jenny out for a drive, Aunt

Sarah was pleased to tell him that Jenny was already out with another admirer.

Gerry went away thoughtfully. Weymouth! A picnic on the beach! He could do better than that or he wasn't the heir to Embury Court. He returned to his rooms and spent a long session on the phone.

Meanwhile the trip to Weymouth was proceeding happily. Alan's old banger certainly gave them a rough ride, but neither cared for that.

'Oh I do like to be beside the seaside!' they sang as they trundled along.

The town was crowded with holiday-makers, but Alan cleverly found a parking space and, clutching their packets of sandwiches, they ran like five-year-olds down to the sea.

'Ice-cream, that's what we need!' exclaimed Alan, paying out extravagantly for two large cornets.

They strolled along the sea front licking their ice-cream, delighted to be just tourists like everybody else.

'I wish I had brought my bikini,' lamented Jenny. 'I could have gone for a swim.'

'Never mind, we can still paddle,' said Alan.

'Brilliant idea!' agreed Jenny.

So when they had licked up the last traces of their cornets, they ran down on the sand to take off their sandals. Alan rolled up his trousers, and they waded in.

'It's glorious!' cried Jenny. 'So cool to the toes.'

'Marvellous!' agreed Alan, splashing happily.

After they had enjoyed the water for a while, Jenny announced that she was getting hungry.

'Right!' said Alan at once. 'We'll have our sandwiches now.'

They waded out, dried their feet on Alan's big handkerchief, and leaning back against a breakwater, munched their simple meal.

'What next?' asked Alan when all was consumed.

'I think I'm going to go to sleep,' said Jenny drowsily.

'Oh no you're not!' cried Alan, jumping up and pulling her to her feet. 'There's lots to see yet.'

'Slave-driver!' laughed Jenny.

Hand in hand they walked along the front to the harbour and admired the yachts anchored there, riding the gentle waves as gracefully as the swans in the bird sanctuary beyond the bridge.

'I'd love to sail away in one of those,' said Jenny.

'Wait till I've made my fortune and I'll hire one just for you,' replied Alan.

'I'm afraid that's going to be a very long wait,' Jenny teased him.

'Oh no it won't!' declared Alan. 'Once my portrait *Girl in Blue Dress* is exhibited my name will be made.'

'You'll owe that to me!' laughed Jenny.

'I know,' he said, suddenly solemn.

Jenny flushed.

'Oh don't let's get serious,' she said. 'We're on holiday.'

'So we are,' he answered quickly. 'Where next?'

'Tea!' exclaimed Jenny, 'I could do with a gallon.'

There were plenty of attractive looking cafés along the front. They chose one and set at a table outside in the sun. Alan ordered a pot of tea for two and then turned to Jenny.

'What else would you like?' he asked. 'Cream cakes?'

'Oh no! What about my figure?'

'There's nothing wrong with your figure that I can see.'

'There will be if I eat cream cakes. I know, I'd like a jam doughnut.'

'Very slimming!' agreed Alan and ordered four.

After this refreshment there was still more to see.

'It says 'Butterfly Farm',' said Jenny, pointing to a large poster. 'Let's go there.'

Twilight was falling when, tired but happy they set off for home. They were too weary to talk or sing on this homeward trip, but were just content to be silent together.

'Thank you, Alan, for a lovely day,' said Jenny as they said good-night.

She stood on tiptoe and kissed his cheek.

He smiled down at her.

'I'm so glad you enjoyed it,' he answered. 'We must do it again.'

'Yes I'd like that,' she said smiling back. 'Good-night.'

Drunk with sun and sea air she happily climbed the winding stair to her tower room. She was soon in bed and dreaming of tropical islands with white sands, blue skies and waving palm trees.

5

'Well?' enquired Aunt Sarah at breakfast the next morning.

'Well what?'

'How did that awful man behave himself?'

'If you mean Alan, I've no complaints. I can't think why you dislike him so.'

'Huh!' answered her aunt cryptically. 'I have my reasons.'

Jenny muttered rebelliously into her cornflakes but mercifully her aunt did not pursue the subject. However when she went out into the garden she had to face more enquiries.

Gerry contrived to meet her on her usual walk round the gardens to breathe the fresh morning air and sniff the perfume of the flowers.

'Did you enjoy Weymouth?' he asked.

'How did you know I went there?'

'Your aunt told me.'

'Nothing's private in this place. No wonder poor Catherine Howard got caught out.'

'Sorry, I didn't know your trip was meant to be secret.'

'It wasn't. It's just that a girl doesn't like to be hounded.'

'Have I been hounding you?'

'No. You've been very circumspect, actually.'

'Good, then you won't mind telling me how you liked Weymouth.'

'I enjoyed every minute. It's a lovely place.'

'I'm glad of that because I was hoping you'd let me take you there.'

'Corned-beef sandwiches on the beach? That doesn't sound like you.'

'It isn't. I've got a much better suggestion. A Cambridge friend of mine has a yacht moored in the harbour.'

'One of those beautiful yachts? Alan and I admired them.'

'Yes, the *White Lady*. He's giving a supper dance aboard on Friday evening.

I've got an invitation. Would you be my partner?'

Jenny's eyes shone.

'I'd be thrilled,' she said.

'So shall I,' answered Gerry, taking her arm.

Jenny removed it firmly.

'I'm not thrilled with you, but with the prospect of going aboard the yacht,' she told him.

Gerry laughed.

'The rest is up to me then,' he said.

Jenny laughed with him, preferring to believe that the veiled threat was a joke.

'I've got to go now,' she said. 'I'm going with Aunt Sarah to hospital to have the plaster taken off her leg.'

'Then we've got a date for Friday,' said Gerry, anxious to make certain of his prize. 'I'll call for you at seven.'

'I'll be ready,' promised Jenny. 'The *White Lady!* I saw her in the harbour. She's magnificent.'

While Aunt Sarah was in the treatment room, Jenny fidgeted some-what impatiently, begrudging the time spent in the stuffy waiting-room, which smelt strongly of disinfectant. At last her aunt hobbled out, leaning heavily on a stick. The plaster was off but the leg was more painful than before when she tried to put her weight upon it. Aunt Sarah was very disappointed for she had thought that once she had got rid of the plaster she would be free to run around like a three-year-old.

'I'm afraid I'm still going to need you, Jenny dear,' she said, desperately clutching on to her niece's arm. 'They say it will take months before I am able to throw this beastly stick away. It makes me feel so ancient.'

'Nonsense, Aunt Sarah,' Jenny reassured her. 'You'll soon be walking normally again as long as you take care. And don't worry about me. Of course I'll stay until the end of my holiday, I'm enjoying myself.'

'I'm so glad dear,' said her aunt, squeezing her hand. 'You've been such a comfort to me. You'll make some lucky man a wonderful wife.'

Jenny laughed carelessly to cover her embarrassment.

'There's no sign of that yet,' she said.

On the drive home, seeking to take her aunt's mind off her aching leg, Jenny told her of the invitation to the supper dance aboard the *White Lady*. The news acted like a strong tonic. Aunt Sarah brightened up at once.

'I'm delighted for you dear,' she cried. 'Do you know I don't think this holiday is going to be wasted after all. I foresee something quite wonderful happening.'

Jenny felt more embarrassed than ever.

'It's only an ordinary hop,' she said.

Aunt Sarah was not to be subdued.

'There's nothing ordinary about Gerald Mountfields,' she said and launched into a pæan of praise as to her favourite's looks, manners and noble breeding. Jenny tried in vain to bring her aunt's soaring imagination down to earth.

'If he's all that he's too good for me,' she laughed.

Aunt Sarah smiled archly and put her hand over Jenny's once again.

'He doesn't think so,' she said.

Jenny heartily wished she had not broached the subject of the supper dance in the confined space of the back of a car whence she could not escape.

Fortunately in the next few days her aunt was too preoccupied with learning to walk again to discuss the virtues of Gerald any further. When Friday evening came Jenny was able to set out in his Porsche without too much of a hassle.

'You look lovely as usual,' Gerry told her as they purred along.

'I've only got this old summer frock,' Jenny apologized. 'I hope it's suitable.'

'Perfect,' replied Gerald putting his hand on her knee.

It was certainly a quicker and more comfortable journey into Weymouth than it had been in Alan's rickety old banger.

Jenny gasped with delight when they reached the harbour. The sea was calm and the *White Lady* rode proudly at anchor. The sun setting behind her threw a rosy glow over her elegant lines. A dinghy bobbed at the quayside in the charge of a stalwart sailor, waiting to convey the guests out to their host and hostess, Michael Grant and his young wife, Penelope.

Gerry helped Jenny tenderly up the rope ladder to the deck and Michael welcomed them rapturously.

'Gerry waxed positively lyrical about you over the phone,' he enthused, holding Jenny's hand much longer than was necessary. While the other guests crowded round to be introduced, Michael slapped Gerry heartily on the back. 'You old reprobate! Trust you to find 'em,' he said.

Jenny flushed with embarrassment, beginning to wish she had not come.

'That's enough of your feeble wit, Mike,' cried Penelope, seeing her guest's confusion. 'Follow me everyone.

Supper is laid down below.'

Jenny followed diffidently. All the other girls were in very tight jeans and scanty tops. She felt very much an unsophisticated schoolmarm in her demure cotton frock.

After a delicious supper of smoked salmon garnished with an exotic salad, and followed by a luscious sweet concoction called 'orange blossoms' Jenny felt better and the admiring glances of the men reassured her. Champagne flowed freely, melting her awkwardness. Mike stood up, rather unsteadily, and raised his glass.

'Ladies and Gentlemen, if there be any such present, drink to the *White Lady*,' he cried.

'The *White Lady*, and all who sail in her,' echoed the assembled company.

This duty accomplished amid cheers and laughter, they all trooped up to the deck and the dancing began. Mike had provided soft romantic music and the boat seemed to rock gently in time to it.

The sun had set now and bright stars shone in a dark blue sky. The sea stretched out to the horizon, a dark mysterious green flecked with white ripples. It was a perfect setting for romance. Jenny's feet scarcely touched the deck as Gerald swung her into the dance, holding her close, his cheek on hers. Lost to earthly reality Jenny floated in a world of fantasy.

The moon had faded and the stars were growing dim when the other dancers began to drift away. Gerald and Jenny still danced on until Mike switched off the music.

'Bedtime, little ones,' he yawned. 'I can offer you a bunk if you like.'

A shock of cold reality woke Jenny from her trance.

'No! No!' she cried. 'Thanks, but I must get home. I've work to do tomorrow.'

'Today,' laughed Mike. 'You're late already.'

'Come on then Gerry. Take me home, please,' ordered Jenny.

'All right, if you insist,' said Gerry reluctantly.

'Thanks Mike for everything. Do the same for you one day.'

In the car driving home, Jenny was silent, her head still in a rosy mist of music and champagne. Gerry smiled to himself in the darkness, but did not disturb her. When at last they purred up to Embury Court he helped her out of the car solicitously and, holding her arm, led her into the garden. The great house was silent, wrapt in slumber. All was in darkness save for the light over the gate-house which gleamed into the shadowed garden and a dim lamp which shone from the Priest's House.

Gerry, having given Jenny a glimpse of a life she had never before known existed, decided that the time had come to claim his reward.

'Thank you Gerry, that was a lovely evening,' she said, and turned to go.

'That's not much of a 'thank you',' he complained.

'What about a kiss?'

Jenny stood on tiptoe and kissed his cheek, just as she had done with Alan.

'Thank you Gerry,' she repeated.

But that was not enough for him. He caught her hands and pulled her to him.

'I want a proper kiss,' he said, and put his mouth on hers.

She yielded for a moment, and then tried to draw away. 'Now I must really go,' she said. 'Good-night.'

'No sweetheart,' he protested, holding her firmly. 'We can't part now. Come up to my rooms. The parents are asleep, we shan't be disturbed.'

'Let me go. I'm not indulging in a sordid affair, creeping like a criminal and pretending.'

'You won't have to creep about. They're all asleep.'

'I would have to crawl out in the morning and pretend to be innocent. I'm not doing that.'

'Oh, come on Jenny! Everyone does these days. It won't be the first time I have had a girl in my room.'

'That's up to them. I'm not telling a lot of lies to my aunt and uncle. Let me go Gerry. You're spoiling a wonderful evening.'

'If you stayed with me it would make it even more wonderful.'

'Oh no it wouldn't!' rasped a voice and a hand shot out and seized Gerry by the collar, wrenching him away from Jenny.

'What the devil?' he shouted. 'Freeman, you bastard! Who asked you to interfere? Get back to the Priest's House and say your prayers!'

'Not until you stop harassing Jenny,' spat Alan. 'She said 'no'. Are you deaf?'

Gerry raised his fists and sent Alan spinning with a blow to the jaw. Alan staggered back, recovered his balance and retaliated with a swinging punch to his rival's solar plexus. The two moved into a clinch and struggled together for the upper hand. It was a combat such as two stags might have engaged in during the rutting season. You could almost hear the clash of horns.

'Stop it!' cried Jenny. 'Stop it at once!'

Inspired by desperation she ran to the stand-pipe used by the gardeners, snatched up the hose and turned it on the combatants. They fell apart, gasping and spluttering.

'I'll not be fought over as though I were a juicy bone!' she shouted. 'I don't want to speak to either of you again. Don't you dare come near me. Neither of you. I hate you both. Goodbye!'

She flung down the hose and, leaving it gushing water over the rivals' feet, ran off towards her tower room.

She was seething with anger. The insolence of it! She was not owned by either of them. When she reached the haven of her room, she sat down on the bed to think things over. She was furious with both her escorts.

'The insolence of Alan!' she thought,' snooping around and spying on her. He must have sat up waiting for her return in order to guard her virtue. It was intolerable; what sort of fool did he think she was? And as for Gerry making a nuisance of himself and refusing to take no for an answer, supposing she would agree to become another of his floozies. The sheer unadulterated gall of it! That was it! She was finished with both of them. She'd come to Embury to help her aunt and uncle and she'd concentrate on that in future.

Still angry, she snatched off her clothes and, leaving them in a heap on the floor, climbed beneath the duvet and fell into a troubled sleep.

She awoke next morning to the monotonous sound of rain dripping off the trees. Clouds had blown up during the night and covered the sun. The world was as grey as her thoughts. Anger still surged through her when she recalled the events of yesterday. What a horrible ending it had been to what had seemed a magical evening. Well, that was that. She had finished with men, all men, the selfish brutes. Henceforth she would devote herself solely to her work with the tourists at Embury Court. This she vowed to herself as she slowly descended the spiral staircase from her tower room to face her aunt's eager enquiries.

Yes, it was a wonderful evening Jenny informed her aunt.

Yes, the yacht was magnificent.

Yes, Gerry was an excellent dancing partner.

'You look pale dear,' Aunt Sarah said at last, after failing to get any really thrilling information out of her niece.

'I expect I'm tired,' Jenny excused herself. 'We got back rather late.'

Jenny was glad that the morning was wet, for that gave her an excuse not to venture into the grounds where those predatory males lurked.

'I'm going to spend the morning in the library,' she told her aunt. 'I want to learn more about those people in the portraits on the main staircase.'

Aunt Sarah, innocently supposing that Gerry would also be studying in the library, smiled upon this plan.

In the quiet of the library, Jenny's

anger began to evaporate. She found some letters describing the chequered life of Lady Frances, the smiling bride who was said to be like herself. Her marriage had not been successful. Her husband had been a brute. Her eldest son, brought forth with much pain, had died in infancy. Jenny began to feel that she herself had nothing of importance to complain about. She decided that she would have to forgive those two idiots who had fought for her favours in the garden. Dolts! What a stupid fuss about nothing.

By the afternoon the wind had blown the clouds away and the rain had cleared. A watery sun appeared. Jenny, pleased with the result of her researches, decided that she needed Alan's help with her plan. She was not going to forgive him, of course. Her approach would be solely a matter of business.

She found him in the midst of his cluttered studio, putting the finishing touches to a view of the gatehouse. He stood up to greet her, holding his palette and paintbrush like a defensive sword and shield.

'Good afternoon, Miss Collins,' he said.

'I'm still not speaking to you,' she said.

'That's perfectly understood,' he answered, keeping a straight face.

'This is purely a matter of business.'

'I shall be delighted to accommodate you if I can.'

'Your black eye looks very painful. That should teach you not to fight.'

'Fight? Who, me? Never! I walked into an open door.'

'How stupid of you. You should look where you're going.'

'I shall do in future. I've learnt my lesson.'

'I'm glad to hear it. Now listen to what I want you to do.'

'I'm all attention.'

'I've mugged up the story of Lady Frances Mountfields. Her portrait's on the main staircase. I want you to do some drawings of her for sale in the shop.'

'Certainly madam. I'll start straight away.'

'Good. I want them for Saturday.'

'You shall have them.'

'That's settled then. What are you doing about that eye?'

'Just being terribly brave.'

'It needs bathing with witch hazel. I'll fetch some from the first-aid cabinet. Put the kettle on while you're waiting.'

By the time Jenny had fussed over Alan's black eye and brewed a restorative pot of tea, all was forgiven and the friendship re-established.

Jenny recounted Lady Frances' story to the tourists at her next guided tour. She was gratified to find it aroused much interest and Alan's sketches sold well.

There was no sign of Gerry. He did not approach Jenny to apologize or complain of his bruises. I expect he's utterly ashamed of himself, thought Jenny. She was wrong. He was busy hatching plans of his own.

6

Some days later Jenny came down to breakfast to find her aunt flushed with excitement, holding a grand-looking invitation card with gold edging.

'It's Gerald's twenty-first birthday next month,' she announced. 'Did he tell you?'

'Not a word.'

'He wanted it to come as a surprise I expect, his parents are giving a big dance and supper party to celebrate. Isn't it exciting?'

'Is it?'

'Of course it is and we're invited! It will be the social event of the year. I must write at once and accept.'

'Leave me out of it. I'm not going.'

'Oh don't be ridiculous Jenny, of course you're going.'

'I don't have to.'

'Now you sound like you did when

you were five and wouldn't eat your greens. I shall accept for all three of us.'

'No, Aunt Sarah. I don't like that sort of grand do.'

'Then you're going to have to put up with it. There'll probably be royalty there. It would be most ill-mannered to refuse.'

'Now you're being ridiculous Aunt Sarah. Royalty won't notice whether I'm there or not.'

'But Lord and Lady Mountfields will. You're forgetting they're your uncle's employers. We're honoured to receive an invitation. It would be extremely rude to refuse.'

'Well, I can't possibly go. I haven't anything suitable to wear.'

'Your uncle and I will soon put that right. We'll go into Dorchester and buy a ballgown for you.'

'Dorchester! You won't get anything worth wearing there.'

'We shall at Madame Francine's.'

'Madame Francine's! She costs the earth!'

'Your uncle will pay. He owes you a lot for your help this summer.'

'I'd rather have the money in my hand to spend as I like.'

'Now stop arguing Jenny. You're just like your mother. She always argued about everything. It's all arranged. We're going into Dorchester this morning. Go and get yourself ready, and you'd better borrow my silk slip. I don't suppose you've got a decent one of your own.'

'No I haven't, I can't afford silk on a schoolmarm's salary.'

'Then go and put mine on and be quick about it. Your uncle will be annoyed if he's kept waiting.'

Resigning herself to the inevitable, Jenny retreated upstairs. Aunt Sarah was unstoppable once she got the bit between her teeth. And a grand social event was just the thing to get her going.

'I'll have to give in with a good grace, I suppose,' she thought. 'But I do regret all that money going into Madame

Francine's pocket instead of mine. At least Gerry will be too much occupied with his rich friends to notice me. I'll cling to the wall and slip out early,' she consoled herself.

She obediently arrayed herself in the silk slip and an easily removable blouse and skirt, and reported for duty downstairs.

'Let's go into Smith and Johnson first,' she suggested, as they walked down Dorchester High Street. 'They're sure to have something that will pass in a crowd at a tenth of Madame Francine's prices.'

'Certainly not,' snapped Aunt Sarah. 'My niece can do better than pass muster in a crowd. We're not going to tiptoe in timidly as though we'd come to mop the floor! I should have thought you'd have more pride.'

'But Aunt Sarah, I can't possibly compete with Gerry's rich friends.'

'Why not? You're prettier than the lot of them.'

'How do you know that? You haven't

seen any of them.'

'I know the type. Now stop arguing for heaven's sake, Jenny. I'm not taking you to the ball dressed by Smith and Johnson! I'd never be able to hold up my head again. And that's final.'

'Oh all right Aunt. It's your money. Come on, let's get it over?'

'I shall never understand you, Jenny,' grumbled her aunt. 'Any other girl would be delighted to be taken into Madame Francine's.'

Thus Jenny stood before the long mirror in the salon, while gowns in bewildering variety were brought forth and draped upon her: gowns in tightly-fitted scarlet satin, long black numbers, slit up to the waist, frothy confections swathed in yards of tulle, sexy wisps of nothing in black lace. She hated them all.

'I look like the dog's dinner,' she complained. 'I'm not aristocratic enough to survive these horrors, it will have to be Smith and Johnson after all.'

Aunt Sarah raised her eyes to heaven in supplication.

'Grant me patience!' she sighed. 'Try on the scarlet again. At least that won't be lost in the crowd.'

Jenny echoed her aunt's sighs and allowed the tight satin to be zipped around her once again.

'I can't breathe,' she complained.

Madame Francine herself, scenting trouble, now swam to the rescue.

'Non! Non! Non!' she shrilled, neatly peeling the scarlet glory from her customer. 'Zat is not for Mademoiselle. Fetch the Pierre Jordan, number twelve, Mavis. Chop chop!'

Pierre Jordan's twelfth inspiration was brought forth and spread before Jenny's enchanted eyes.

The gown was of white silk embroidered with tiny blue and green flowers. The full skirt fell from a deep, close-fitting basque, from which sprung the low vee-neck line and wide cap sleeves. It was Pierre Jordan's masterpiece.

Madam Francine slipped it over

Jenny's head and tied the sash tightly behind her waist so that the basque fitted smoothly over her hips. Jenny twirled in front of the long mirror, smiling at her own flower-like reflection.

'Younger than springtime!' cooed Madame Francine, putting her hand over the price tag.

'We'll take it,' said Aunt Sarah decisively as though afraid that this magical vision might be snatched away from her. Uncle Henry was called in to survey the metamorphosis of his favourite schoolmarm into Cinderella arrayed for the ball. He got out his cheque book and paid without wincing.

Jenny flung her arms round him and kissed him.

'You're the most wonderful uncle a girl ever had,' she cried.

Aunt Sarah sighed with relief. The tiresome child would be dressed as befitted her youth and beauty, and all she had to do now was to sit back and await developments. It had been a struggle, but she had triumphed as usual.

Now that she had this delightful garment to wear, Jenny's attitude to the forthcoming celebrations softened. She began positively to look forward to it. So that when she met Gerry in the garden she smiled upon him kindly. He responded with alacrity.

'I'm so glad you're coming to my birthday bash,' he said. 'Does that mean I'm forgiven?'

'Life's too short for vendettas,' she responded. 'Provided of course you apologize humbly.'

He immediately knelt upon the damp grass and knocked his head three times upon the ground.

'Forgive me, O Queen,' he intoned.

'Get up, you oaf,' laughed Jenny, kicking him. 'I suppose it's useless expecting you to be sensible.'

'I couldn't be more serious,' he grinned, scrambling to his feet. 'May I have the first dance?'

'Don't be daft! You'll have all the

VIPs to escort. Besides I've already promised it to a more deserving partner.'

'Not that rat Freeman?'

'For heaven's sake don't start all that up again, or I'll not dance with you at all. No, my uncle's leading me out, of course. He's much more charming than you two squabbling schoolboys.'

'You are hard, my Queen,' he answered. 'Very well if I can't have the first dance, I'll have the second.'

'No you won't, I'll put you down for number thirteen. Cheerio and the best of luck.'

This exchange invigorated Jenny and she joined with her aunt in watching with excitement the preparations for the ball.

The gardeners bent their backs to make sure that the grounds looked their best. Fairy-lights were strung from tree to tree, and Chinese lanterns adorned the terraces. Uncle Henry was called to supervise the decoration of the ball-room. Caterers' and florists' vans sped up and down the drive. Electricians trailed their cables upstairs into the drawing-room and downstairs into the cellars. There were to be two bands: prestigious Luigi Balon's Orchestra in the ballroom; Don Juan and his Jungle Drummers in the cellar. Both had to be wired for sound.

Aunt Sarah flung herself into the furore making helpful suggestions and generally getting in the way of the flower-arrangers. Jenny was called upon to stand back and admire the results.

Alan was the only inhabitant of the castle to appear uninterested in the excitement. He took his easel to the far side of the lake and concentrated on the daunting task of translating the tranquil water on to a canvas. Jenny, taking a quiet walk to clear her head, which was whirling from all the bustle, found him there.

'So this is where you're hiding,' she said, collapsing on the grass beside him.

'I'm not hiding. I'm working,' he replied.

'Beg your pardon, my mistake,' said

Jenny, kneeling up to survey the painting.

'I like that! It's very good,' she exclaimed.

'I know.'

'It's your modesty which wins friends and influences people.'

'I know that too. That's why I have to escape from my admirers to search for peace!'

'There will be no peace at Embury Court for the next few days. Are you coming to the shindig on Saturday?'

'Have I got a choice? I thought it was a royal command.'

'It's exactly that according to Aunt Sarah.'

Alan sighed heavily.

'Oh well, I suppose I shall have to haul my dinner jacket out of the old tin trunk.'

'And polish your shoes,' said Jenny, looking at the disreputable trainers on his feet.

'I'll do even that if you'll dance with me.'

'Do you know how to dance?'

'Well I can twist and twirl until my poor old back gives out I suppose. Are you going to take pity on me?'

'I make no promises. I'll wait and see how well you've polished your shoes.'

'Oh, but you must dance with me. You'll be the only person there that I know.'

'You're making me cry. You could have thought of a more romantic way of asking me to dance.'

'I don't feel very romantic about Birthday Boy's Hallelujah Chorus.'

'What would you feel romantic about?' asked Jenny hastily, to steer him away from his dislike of Gerry.

'A plate of steak-and-kidney pudding like my granny used to make with carrots and new potatoes, and apple pie and custard to follow.'

'All you'd want to do after that would be to go to sleep.'

'And what beautiful romantic dreams I should have!'

'You're hopeless! A dead loss to all

women. I'll leave you to commune with the ducks and go back to my flower-arranging,' said Jenny, scrambling to her feet. 'Cheerio.'

'Don't forget your promise,' Alan called after her. 'My shoes will shine so brightly they'll dim the Chinese lanterns.'

Jenny returned to her aunt's side much refreshed.

Alan was an absolute idiot. He was serious about nothing but his painting. She could not think why she liked him. Nevertheless her headache had vanished.

★ ★ ★

At last the big night arrived. The fairy-lights lit up the gardens, throwing mysterious shadows over the alleys, and the Chinese lanterns on the terrace glowed a welcome. Rolls Royces, Peugeots and similar luxurious vehicles crunched up the wide drive to the gate-house. Romantic music from Luigi Balon and his Orchestra wafted out on the summer air.

Jenny, looking delightful in flowered silk, arrived on her uncle's arm. Gerry's eyes lit up when he saw this lovely vision, and so did the eyes of many another young man. Jenny contrived to blush modestly, and when they had paid their respects to their host and hostess, the little party from the East Tower retired to a seat by the open french windows.

Jenny now had leisure to look around and observe her fellow guests. Being only an ignorant schoolmarm unused to the high life, she was astonished to see that the aim of the other young women guests was to be outrageous rather than beautiful. The competition was fierce. Long black nightdresses vied for attention with wisps of satin apparently held in place by chewing-gum. There were diaphanous Turkish trousers, tight striped bodystockings and fringed lampshades worn with an air of self-satisfaction. Hair was either artfully tangled or gummed into strange shapes that nature never knew. Ear-rings were enormous and, in Jenny's eyes, uniformly hideous.

'Well!' exclaimed Aunt Sarah. 'If you can't beat that lot I'll — well really I don't know what I'll do.'

'But I don't want to beat them, Aunt Sarah,' said Jenny. 'I'm happy as I am.'

'So I should think,' snapped back her aunt. 'Your gown is absolutely right for this occasion — what are you laughing at Henry?'

'Nothing dear. Just a thought. Come on Jenny, let's dance,' and he proudly led his beautiful niece out on to the floor.

'What a crew!' he whispered as they twirled.

'They're aristocrats Uncle, and rich enough to get away with it.'

'Then for the first time in my life I'm glad we're only ordinary,' decided Henry.

'I think it's rather fun,' said Jenny. 'But I do grudge all that money you spent on this old-fashioned fairytale dress!'

However she was soon to change her mind. When Gerry had done his duty by his very important guests, he made a beeline for Jenny and claimed his promised dance.

'You're the most beautiful girl here,' he told her as he took her in his arms and steered her out into the middle of the floor.

Jenny bit back the sharp retort that rose to her lips and smiled demurely.

'Thank you,' she said.

Their steps fitted perfectly, as they had done on the yacht at Weymouth. They danced on, oblivious of all but the rhythm of the music.

Aunt Sarah watched them proudly. She had been right after all, as she always was. That gown was worth every penny.

Other watchers were not so pleased. Lord and Lady Mountfields looked with disfavour on Gerry's partner. A pretty little thing no doubt, but not what they had in mind for their son and heir.

Alan also watched their progress with dismay. Then he turned away sorrowful. She had found her millionaire. He left the party and went back to the Priest's House. There he pulled off his dinner jacket and shining dance shoes. All that polishing for nothing! He clothed himself again in his comfortable old jeans and pullover.

'Ah well!' he consoled himself. 'There is still painting. Far better to keep women out of your life. They only mess things up.'

Whistling a merry tune he began to mix up paint ready for the morrow.

7

So effective indeed had been the flowered ballgown, that there now began for Jenny a whirlwind romance. It seemed that Gerry had fallen for her seriously and was determined to win her. He wooed and pursued her with persistence and style.

His first ploy was to introduce her to the joys of riding. He persuaded her to join him in an early morning ride across the park. Jenny had never ridden before, and he chose for her a broad-backed mare suitable for a beginner. He cantered round her on his own spirited filly, laughing at the way she clutched at Buttercup's mane. Stung by his laughter, Jenny soon conquered her fear and sat upright, boldly trotting over the turf.

'Enjoying yourself?' asked Gerry.

'It's wonderful. I'm hooked.'

'It's time you relaxed,' he told her. 'You're far too serious for one so beautiful. You look magnificent on a horse. You've got a natural seat.'

Jenny warmed to his flattery. The sun continued to shine and all was right with the world.

In the evenings, Gerry's rakish two-seater was brought up to consolidate the attack. Jenny was whizzed away from Embury Court and all thought of tourists and conducted tours. She was wined and dined in various expensive places. Her feet scarcely touched the ground.

Aunt Sarah was all triumphant smiles, and Uncle Henry also smiled, pleased to see his favourite niece so happy.

In the private apartments of the Mountfields, however, smiles were few. There were councils of war behind closed doors, and long conversations on the transatlantic telephone. As a result a high-powered Mercedes glided up the drive carrying a visitor and her extensive luggage.

That same afternoon Jenny was invited to take tea on the terrace with Lord and Lady Mountfields.

'That's wonderful Jenny dear,' crowed Aunt Sarah. 'The Mountfields have accepted you as Gerald's special friend.'

'Yes, I think they have,' smiled Jenny. 'I must put on my best frock for the occasion. I feel as though I'm being interviewed for a job.'

'Perhaps you are, a very important job too,' hinted Aunt Sarah mysteriously.

Thus, arrayed in her best frock, the blue one, Jenny mounted the terrace steps to where Lady Mountfields sat in state behind her silver tea service. The greeting Jenny received was polite but chilly.

'Do sit down,' she was told, with no appended endearment. But this did not matter to Jenny, for Gerry rose to greet her, conducted her to a seat in the cool shade and fetched her a cup of tea.

'You look lovely, as usual,' he

whispered as he did so.

'Cake?' he asked, making the word a caress.

'Just a simple biscuit,' smiled Jenny.

'As you wish, but you don't need to diet,' he grinned. He sat himself on a low stool at her feet and continued to pay her absurd compliments. Jenny sipped her tea in contentment. All was well with the world.

Suddenly, without any warning, that world was turned topsy-turvy. There appeared, framed in the open french windows, a radiant vision in a beautifully cut silk sundress which must have cost hundreds. Her reception was in sickening contrast to that accorded to Jenny.

'There you are, Leila, dear!' cried Lady Mountfields, holding out a be-ringed hand. 'Come and sit by me. Did you find everything you needed?'

Lord Mountfields leapt to his feet and solicitously conducted the vision to a cushioned basket-chair. She smiled her gracious acknowledgement and settled herself elegantly.

'Leila!' cried Gerry also leaping up. 'Where did you spring from?'

'I didn't spring, I flew,' said Leila, holding up her face for a kiss.

He responded enthusiastically.

'Why didn't you come to my birthday bash?' he demanded.

'Sheer folly,' smiled Leila. She looked around her appreciatively. 'I had forgotten it was so lovely here.'

'Well, now you're here at last, we all hope you'll stay for a long time,' purred Lady Mountfields.

Jenny was left awkwardly clutching her cup and saucer, and gaping at the newcomer. She was not beautiful, but seemed so because of the skilful way she presented herself. Her clothes were the best that money could buy, and her dark hair was cunningly cut to appear naturally wavy. Her bare legs were slim and attractively tanned. On her feet were Italian-made sandals of white kid. Her best feature was her eyes, which were of an unusual green. These she had emphasized with careful make-up. Sensing Jenny's scrutiny, she looked across at her.

'Do introduce me to your friend, Gerry,' she said.

'Sorry, I forgot,' said Gerry. Jenny Collins — Leila Barton.'

Jenny twisted her lips into a smile of greeting.

'Are you on holiday, Jenny?' asked Leila in friendly fashion.

'Well, sort of,' said Jenny.

'Miss Collins is our curator's niece,' explained Lady Mountfields. 'She's down here to help conduct the tourists round the public rooms.'

'How brave of you Jenny,' smiled Leila. 'Aren't you terrified?'

'Not at all. The tourists are human. They don't bite.'

'Miss Collins is a schoolteacher,' interposed Lady Mountfields. 'She's used to that sort of thing.'

'Oh, of course!' agreed Leila. 'A few tourists must hold no terrors for her.'

Their voices had a derogatory ring as

118

though this honoured profession were inhabited only by middle-aged viragos in high-necked blouses and pince-nez. They looked across at Jenny in condescending fashion. She was one of the lower orders obviously.

'You are too pretty to be a schoolmarm,' said Leila, sweetly patronizing.

Jenny felt bereft of words.

'Thanks,' she choked. She did not know how to deal with this studied insolence.

Digging her nails into her palms to prevent herself screaming, she stood up.

'Well, I'm afraid I must be going,' she said. 'Things to do. Thank you so much for your hospitality, Lady Mountfields.'

She turned and ran down the terrace steps, desperate to get away. Gerry, recalled to his duty, followed her.

'I'll see you home,' he said.

'There's no need,' Jenny told him. 'I can find my way across the garden without a map.'

'Right then, I'll see you tomorrow morning at the stables.'

'OK,' said Jenny, pretending unconcern. She did not remind him that they had arranged to go out together that evening.

She did not feel she could face her Aunt Sarah's probing questions, so she ran through the archway and along the winding path to the lake. She sat down on the grass, trying to subdue her fury at the patronizing treatment she had received. A little family of ducks came swimming over to her hoping she had something tasty for them.

'Hullo,' she said. 'You don't know how lucky you are. All you care about is food.'

She did not notice Alan approaching from the opposite side of the lake. He came and sat down on the grass beside her.

'What's wrong?' he asked.

'Nothing whatever. Why should there be? I'm talking to the ducks, that's all.'

'Oh, I just thought you looked hot and bothered.'

'It's a hot day.'

'True,' he agreed, and gazed out over the lake in silent sympathy.

'I've just been taking tea with Lord and Lady Mountfields,' Jenny burst out at last.

'Enough to make anyone want to talk to ducks.'

'They've got an apparently very dear friend staying with them — Leila Barton.'

'I've heard of her. Stinking rich and often in the gossip columns.'

'Do you read the gossip columns then?'

'I have to keep an eye on the clientele. Her dad's rolling in the stuff. He owns Barton's Supermarkets and he fancies himself as an art connoisseur. I shall have to contrive to meet our Leila and try to persuade her to tell Dad she's found a genius in the wilds of Dorset.'

'You'll love her. She's fascinating.'

'Oh, but I was planning on fascinating her!'

'You haven't a hope.'

'So you don't rate my powers of fascination very highly?'

'Sorry.'

'Then I'll have to fall back on my 'little boy lost' ploy. She won't be able to resist tidying my studio and washing my shirt.'

Jenny could not help laughing at Alan's nonsense. The vision of the elegant Leila condescending to wash Alan's shirt was irresistible.

'So you don't think that will work either?'

'No I don't.'

'Then I'll have to knock myself over the head and lie across her path groaning and pleading for help.'

'She'll step over you!' laughed Jenny.

Their laughter was balm to Jenny's hurt spirit. The baleful witch she had met on the terrace shrank to no more than a posturing young woman with too high an opinion of herself.

The next morning Jenny jumped out of bed, eager for the promised canter round the park. She pulled on her ancient jeans and a tee-shirt and ran down to the stables. She found, much to her dismay, that Leila was before her, arrayed in beautifully tailored jodhpurs.

'Hullo,' Jenny said. 'Are you joining us?'

'I was just going to ask you the same question.'

'Why, is this a permanent date with Gerry?'

'No, just a canter round the park.'

Jenny busied herself saddling Buttercup, the steady old mare which had given her such uncomplaining support. Leila turned to the groom in attendance.

'Johnson,' she ordered, 'saddle up Chieftain, for me.'

The groom looked doubtful.

'He's very frisky this morning, Miss,' he warned.

'That's all right. I can handle him,' said Leila.

'What's this?' enquired Gerry, putting in a belated appearance. 'Did I hear Chieftain mentioned?'

'You did. I have milord's permission to ride him.'

'He can deny you nothing,' grinned Gerry.

'You'll do the same if you know what's good for you, you wolf. What are you up to, dating two women at once?'

'Why? Are you girls quarrelling over me already?'

'You're getting above yourself my lad. This pretty little thing has been too soft with you.'

'Yes. And we've enjoyed every minute, haven't we Jenny, darling?'

'It's been sheer heaven.'

Leila's green eyes flashed. She was getting the worst of the exchange and did not like it.

'Heaven's a little precarious these days,' she snapped. 'It's very easy to fall through the hole in the ozone layer.'

Gerry laughed and winked at Jenny. She winked in return, feeling reassured.

'Come on then girls,' cried Gerry. 'Boots, spurs, to horse and away!'

Jenny clambered happily on to

Buttercup's broad back. Leila had been subdued easily enough. Her triumph was short-lived. As soon as they had trotted out into the park, Leila slapped her whip against Chieftain's flank.

'Race you to the spinney!' she cried.

'Oh no you don't!' answered Gerry. 'A fiver that I'll be at the gate first!'

He whipped up his own mount and the two galloped off into the distance, leaving Jenny trailing dismally behind on dear old Buttercup. She cantered sedately around for a while and then took the horse back, to the stables. She did not want to meet the renegades coming back, but she need not have worried. The thoughtless pair had disappeared into the depths of the spinney.

Her dismal outing concluded, Jenny managed to nip up to her room without encountering her aunt. She changed quickly into a cotton frock and wandered out into the gardens, feeling at a loss. Her feet, seemingly without her volition, strayed in the direction of the Priest's House.

Alan was sitting outside sketching the snake fountain.

'Hullo,' he said. 'Have you come to make my coffee?'

'Is that all I'm good for?'

'There's a couple of doughnuts in the tin. Can a man do more than offer his last doughnut?'

Jenny stood behind him and surveyed his sketch.

'What do you think?' he asked. 'Moving water is always a challenge.'

'You deserve coffee,' decided Jenny. 'I'll get it for you.'

'Ministering angel!' said Alan absently, putting his head on one side and squinting at his picture.

Jenny brought out the coffee and doughnuts and sat down on the steps of the fountain.

'Had a good ride?' asked Alan.

'Marvellous.'

'Good, seen anything of Miss Leila Moneybags?'

'Not a lot. These doughnuts are stale.

How long have you had them?'

'Oh I don't know, about a week I suppose.'

'Ug! They're not even fit for the ducks.'

'You're too fussy. Personally I like my doughnuts stale,' said Alan manfully, chewing at his lump of concrete. 'Not a bad morning's work, I think. Not brilliant but passable. Definitely one for my exhibition. Your portrait will be the centre-piece of course, but I wish I had another work of genius to back it up.'

'I suppose you have to be inspired to produce one of those?'

'But where else can inspiration be found in this wilderness? Two pictures of you would be a touch monotonous.'

Jenny swallowed hard, and then made the supreme sacrifice.

'Shall I bring you the loaded Leila?' she asked.

'Do you reckon she'll inspire me?'

'Bound to.'

'Can you really lure her into my parlour?'

'I have ways.'

'I always knew you were an angel. Didn't I say so? By the way where is the quarry?'

'She was last seen disappearing into the spinney.'

'Then she's probably lost. I must go at once and rescue her,' said Alan, not moving.

'That wouldn't be appreciated. She's got Gerry with her.'

'Poor little rich girl! In that case she's doubly in need of rescuing.'

Jenny laughed a little sourly.

'I doubt it,' she said. 'It's more likely to be Gerry who's in need of rescuing.'

'Serve him right, the fat-headed basket. I shan't bother. He'll have to find a couple of rabbits to help him. Got any more coffee? This doughnut is taking some chewing.'

Alan's light-hearted attitude to what had seemed an intolerable humiliation to Jenny, helped her regain her balance. She went back to the house with a smile on her face, ready to confront her aunt's probing queries.

Late that afternoon when Jenny was ushering out a little band of tourists, Gerry approached her.

'Sorry about this morning,' he said.

'Why? What did you do?' asked Jenny, feigning unconcern.

'Galloped off and left you. I thought you'd be angry.'

'Not in the least. Buttercup and I were quite happy on our own.'

'Nice of you to take it that way. You see I've got to entertain Leila. She's an old friend.'

'Naturally. She's such a charming girl. You must look after your guests. Don't give it another thought. I'm afraid I must hurry after my flock now. I want to steer them round the Gift Shop. Cheerio!'

Gerry looked after her gaping. This careless response was disconcerting. He had expected tearful recriminations followed by a cosy session of kiss and make up. Jenny marched into the Gift Shop after her tourists with her head held high and a bitter smile twisting her lips. She was disappointed and disillusioned. She vowed she would never trust romantic overtures again.

8

Aunt Sarah was even more disappointed than Jenny. 'What has happened to Gerry these days?' she asked with a worried frown.

'The Mountfields have got guests,' Jenny explained. 'He's been roped in to entertain them.'

The plural was not a lie, she excused herself. Leila was equal to three at least.

Leila indeed was inescapable. She seemed to Jenny to infest every corner of the estate, even penetrating the Gift Shop.

When Jenny was escorting the last of a party of tourists from the shop, Leila swept in as though she were already Lady Mountfields. She inspected the mementoes laid out to trap the unwary. Mugs, bookmarks and keyrings, all bearing a picture of the ancient house, came under her scrutiny. She enquired of the sales manageress as to profits and outlay in a charming way which had a hint of steel beneath. The manageress was eager to oblige her, not knowing her exact status.

When she came to Alan's pictures, she stopped short, genuinely interested at last. She picked up his portrait of Lady Caroline, and held it up at arm's length.

'This is remarkably good,' she pronounced.

'They sell well,' fussed the manageress.

'So I should think, at this price. They're worth three times as much.'

'We find this is the most viable price,' explained the manageress.

'We shouldn't get anyone to pay three times as much,' interposed Jenny. 'Funds are limited even among the Americans, and the Japanese are very careful with their money.'

'They're getting bargains,' said Leila. 'These pictures will be worth a lot in the future.'

'Yes, I think they're pretty good too,'

agreed Jenny. 'The artist is staying here you know.'

'I must meet this so modest artist,' said Leila. 'Lead me to his garret.'

'Right. This way,' said Jenny with a feeling of triumph. 'Follow me into his parlour,' she muttered beneath her breath. 'The too modest spider awaits the juicy fly.'

As they threaded their way through the flower-beds, Leila paused beneath a rose arbour.

'Let's sit here a minute,' she said.

Jenny sat obediently.

'I hope we're not going to quarrel,' said Leila.

'Why should we?'

'Well I suppose I've spoilt your little game.'

'Game?'

'Yes, Gerry must seem quite a catch to an unsophisticated little school-teacher.'

Jenny choked. She clenched and unclenched her hands struggling to control her fury. Nothing she could say seemed adequate.

'Oh ah!' she gulped.

'I just want things straight between us. You'll have to fade away now. Concentrate on your tourists. I am going to marry Gerry.'

'Does he know that?'

'Not yet. That pleasure's to come.'

'Maybe he'll turn you down.'

'I shouldn't advise you to hope for that. He may be a bit scatter-brained, but he's not a fool.'

'Um!'

'It's a perfect match. My money and his inheritance. It was made in heaven.'

'But what about love?'

'Love! I finished with that when I was seventeen.'

'How sad!'

Leila laughed and smiled down at Jenny.

'I like you,' she said. 'You're so refreshingly old-fashioned.'

'I'm just ordinary.'

'Far from it dear. I couldn't understand what Gerry saw in you at first. It must have been the novelty.'

'Poor Gerry!'

'Rubbish! He's remarkably lucky, and he knows it. Well, I'm glad we've got that straight,' said Leila rising briskly and smoothing down her elegant slacks. 'Come along, let's get to the garret.'

Leila looked round Alan's chaotic studio with amused appreciation.

'What a superb garret!' she exclaimed.

'I do my best,' replied Alan, endeavouring to look charmingly unconventional.

Leila then proceeded to tour the paintings propped up round the walls. When she came to the portrait of Jenny, she stopped short and examined it carefully, her head on one side.

'That's extraordinarily good,' she said.

'I know,' said the modest artist.

'I'd like you to paint me.'

'Are you offering me a commission?'

'Of course.'

'I don't come cheap.'

'I don't require anything cheap.'

'Then I accept.'

'That's settled then. Where would be the best background?'

'The snake fountain,' suggested Jenny.

'No, no!' answered Alan, suppressing a smile. 'Miss Barton is not an outdoor subject. Within the gate-house, perhaps? No, I have it, the Pink Drawing-room, of course.'

Leila smiled, delighted at this suggestion. 'Ideal,' she exclaimed.

'But you'd have to get Lord Mountfields' permission first,' said Jenny, thinking of the interruption to her tours.

'Oh I can arrange that,' said Leila calmly. 'That's no problem. What should I wear?'

Alan surveyed her, noting especially her unusual green eyes.

'Black velvet,' he decided. 'How are your legs?'

'They've been much admired.'

'Good. Then a full skirt, mid-calf length. Wide sleeves to fall gracefully

136

from your arms. Yes, I begin to see it.'

'I have just the garment,' smiled Leila. 'How fortunate.'

'I start early,' warned Alan. 'Nine o'clock in the Pink Drawing-room. I'll have my easel set up. I'll see you then and not a second later.'

'I'll be there,' promised Leila, an expression of smug delight on her face.

'The hell-begotten harridan!' exploded Jenny, as soon as Leila was out of sight.

'Why? What's she done to you?'

'Been unbelievably insolent! She called me refreshingly old-fashioned.'

'That sounds to me like a compliment,' said Alan annoyingly.

'And she actually had the cheek to warn me off Gerry.'

'That sounds like good advice.'

'Whose side are you on?'

'I'm just an unbiased observer.'

'Huh! You're just trying to wind me up, you swine!'

'It seems to me that you're pretty well wound up already. A nice strong cup of tea is what you want, and I've got a fresh supply of doughnuts.'

'You make it,' said Jenny, collapsing on to a packing-case. 'I haven't the strength.'

The tea Alan brought her was strong and sweet. Jenny gulped it down gratefully.

'Oh poor Gerry!' she mourned, swallowing a large chunk of doughnut.

'Why? What's he done, fallen off his horse and broken his neck?'

'Worse. Leila says she's going to marry him.'

'Serve him right.'

'But Alan, she's buying him! She told me herself.'

'She's not buying Gerry, my dear, she's buying Embury Court.'

'Oh, my poor, lovely, doomed Embury! She'll ruin it!'

'Have another doughnut,' suggested Alan.

However matters did not turn out exactly as Leila had planned. Whilst she was immured with Alan in the Pink Drawing-room, Gerald was free to seek out Jenny. He found her in the library following the adventures of an Elizabethan Mountfields who had earned himself a nice little fortune and the gratitude of his queen from piracy on the high seas against the Spanish treasure ships.

'Hullo!' Gerry said. 'I've been searching for you. So this is where you're hiding.'

'Not hiding, working.'

'Work? I wouldn't know about that.'

'But aren't you supposed to be reading for the bar?'

Gerry shuddered.

'What a wicked thing to say to a delicate lad. The bar can wait. I'm busy gathering rosebuds.'

'You'll have to give up your idle ways once you're married.'

'Married?'

'Yes, aren't you engaged to Leila?'

'No. Who told you that?'

'She did.'

'She was having you on.'

'Warning me off more like.'

'Rubbish! It must have been her idea of a joke. She's got an odd sense of humour.'

'Very odd!'

'That's enough chit-chat. I'm going over to Denton Country Club for a swim. They've got a superb pool. Care to join me?'

'It's a tempting idea.'

'Always give in to temptation,' quoted Gerry.

Jenny laughed and shut the volume she had been studying with a bang.

'Right,' she said, jumping up. 'I'll fetch my towel.'

Delighted to escape from the sombre library, she skipped happily across the courtyard and up the winding stairs to her room. Snatching up her swimming gear, she ran lightly down again and put her head round the kitchen door.

'Cheer up, Auntie!' she called. 'I'm going swimming with Gerry.'

He proudly handed her into his open-topped Jaguar, the very latest model which his parents had given him on his coming of age. They sped off down the country lanes, putting all cares behind them. Gerry put his foot down and careered round every twist and turn, sending frightened sheep galloping away into safer corners. Jenny too was much relieved when they turned safely into the entrance of the Country Club.

The Denton pool was indeed superb. Set in a ring of carefully nurtured palm trees, its blue water sparkled in the sunlight, conjuring up a vision of a beach in the Bahamas. A number of young people, equally carefree, were gathered round the pool, splashing in the water or lazing on loungers round the edges.

Jenny and Gerry changed quickly, eager to join in the fun. Gerry ostentatiously showed off his diving from the top board. Jenny displayed her figure from the spring-board. They both thoroughly enjoyed themselves. When they grew tired they stretched themselves luxuriously beside the pool, sipping long drinks, happily relaxed after the exercise.

A burly young man approached Gerry with a theatrical air of menace.

'Where have you been you old reprobate?' he demanded.

'Studying hard, of course,' retorted Gerry.

'Liar!'

'What do you want, you big baboon?' asked Gerry. 'Can't you see I'm trying to rest in peace?'

The young man turned to Jenny with an ingratiating smile.

'I'm Dave Brewster,' he said. 'Aren't you the girl in the flowered dress at Gerry's shindig? I was manoeuvring to get a dance with you all the evening, but the selfish hound wouldn't let me get near.'

'And you can keep away from her now,' snapped Gerry. 'Jenny's with me.'

'What a way to treat an old friend?' complained Dave. 'And I was going to invite you to the Aero Club to give you a whirl.'

'Aero Club!' said Jenny. 'That sounds exciting.'

'It will be I promise you. What about tomorrow?'

'Well,' replied Jenny. 'I can't promise, you'll have to fix it up with Gerry.'

'Why bother with him? I'll come over to Embury Court and fetch you myself.'

'Don't you dare! You'll get a bucket of boiling oil on your head,' warned Gerry.

'Sorry, Dave,' said Jenny. 'You see how it is. The young master keeps me locked up in a tower.'

'The fiend! But I suppose we'll have to put up with him until I can think of a plan to rescue you. I'll see you both at the Aero Club then. The spin is arranged for eleven a.m. Be prompt I want to start on schedule.'

'If you're lucky,' replied Gerry.

'If I'm not I'll be over with a battering ram and a rope ladder,' laughed Dave.

'I'm afraid I can't promise,' repeated Jenny.

'If you don't come you'll break my heart,' declared Dave.

When they neared Embury, Gerry stopped the car on top of the hill where a beautiful oak tree spread its branches. He climbed out and stretched out his hand to help Jenny to follow.

'Come and look,' he said. 'There's a wonderful view from here.'

Jenny obeyed, maybe not quite so innocently as she pretended, and he took her in his arms. She lifted her face to his and he kissed her long and hard.

'It's not only Dave's heart that will be broken if you don't come tomorrow,' he said.

'I make no promises,' answered Jenny, teasingly.

He rewarded her with several even more passionate kisses.

'What must I do to persuade you?' he asked.

'Behave yourself,' laughed Jenny, trying to push him away.

But he would not release her.

'I shan't let you go until you've kissed me in return,' he said.

Jenny stood on tiptoe and pecked his cheek.

'Come on, you can do better than that,' he said, holding her tighter.

'If I do will you promise to let me go?'

'Scout's honour.'

So Jenny pulled his head down and put her mouth on his.

'Magic!' gasped Gerry, coming up for air. 'I knew you had hidden fires.'

But he kept his word and dutifully handed her back to the car.

By the time the truants returned home Leila had finished her session with Alan. When she saw their glowing faces and damp hair, her green eyes flashed, but her lips twisted into a smile.

'Thanks Jenny, for keeping Gerry out of mischief,' she said.

'It was a pleasure,' smiled Jenny.

'I've got another session with Alan tomorrow. Will you be going swimming again?' asked Leila kindly as though to a little child.

This patronizing attitude decided Jenny.

'Not tomorrow,' she said. 'I'll be in a whirl tomorrow.'

The next day Jenny and Gerry sneaked out of Embury Court like truants from school. They laughed gleefully as they sped through the country lanes. The fact that they had cunningly kept this adventure secret made it all the more thrilling.

Dave greeted them exuberantly, and led them to a yellow helicopter, which was waiting on the launching pad as though eager to be off.

'Whacko!' he cried, thumping Gerry on the back. 'Welcome aboard.'

'Where's the pilot?' asked Gerry.

'*C'est moi*, of course,' said Dave. 'Are you scared?'

'Terrified if you're going to be in charge.'

'Oh ye of little faith! Do you want to see my licence?'

'What's the use? It's probably forged.'

'Oh come on Gerry,' urged Jenny. 'Of course he's qualified or they wouldn't let him have a helicopter.'

'A girl after my own heart! I knew it when I first set eyes on you,' cried Dave, handing Jenny into the helicopter with the utmost solicitude. 'Let's fly off without him.'

'Oh no you don't,' retorted Gerry, climbing in after them. 'If we've got to die, we'll die together.'

'You are an idiot,' expostulated Jenny. 'It can't be more hair-raising than a ride in your Jaguar.'

'Well said,' agreed Dave climbing into the pilot's seat. 'Hold tight. We're off.'

He set the rotors whirling and the helicopter rose slowly into the air and circled gracefully round the airfield.

'Tell all my friends I forgive them,' moaned Gerry, pretending terror and seizing the excuse to clasp Jenny's hand.

'Oh shut up Gerry,' said Jenny. 'I

want to enjoy the view.'

But she did not withdraw her hand.

The prospect stretched out beneath the helicopter was indeed pleasing seen from on high. The farms, barns and houses shrank to a doll-like size, and the road stretched like a ribbon between the fields. All ugliness and decay were merged by distance into an ever-changing panorama of greens, browns and soft reds.

'I'm loving this,' exclaimed Jenny. 'Where are you taking us?'

'Just for a whirl,' answered Dave. 'You'll see.'

They flew on over hill and dale until the seashore came in sight, lapped by a fringe of white surf, and bobbing with sail-boards and bathers. Dave dipped down low and the holiday crowds gazed up at them and waved. Jenny enthusiastically waved back.

'This is fun,' she said.

'Come on Gerry,' laughed Dave. 'Express your appreciation. Don't be shy. Am I such a villain after all?'

'You'll pass in a crowd,' grinned Gerry.

Dave swung the machine round and flew inland again. After a while the territory became familiar, and the red brick walls and towers of Embury Court came in sight.

'Here you are Gerry,' he said. 'I thought you'd like a survey of your realm.'

'Good thinking!' said Gerry. 'So you have got some brains after all.'

Dave flew round the park, making the deer run in fright, and over the gardens and house.

'Oh I do love Embury!' cried Jenny.

'So do I,' said Gerry, serious for once.

He put his arm round her and for a few minutes they were at one in their affection for the ancient manor.

Dave flew round once more and then set off back to the air-field. When they had landed both Jenny and Gerry tried to thank him. But he would have none of it.

'The show's not over yet,' he said, 'you're having lunch with me.'

'Decent of you to offer,' replied Gerry, 'but I'm afraid I've got to get back.'

'Come on Gerry!' expostulated Dave. 'I accepted your hospitality, now you're got to accept mine.'

'That's true!' said Jenny, throwing caution to the wind.

'This way folks,' said Dave ushering his guests towards the restaurant.

It was an exhilarating meal for Jenny. She blossomed beneath the admiring glances of these two personable young men.

'Thanks Dave. I have enjoyed myself,' she said when it was over, and she rashly kissed him.

'My pleasure,' he replied, holding her close.

'Now it's time for home,' she said, neatly extricating herself.

'That's right,' said Gerry, tucking his arm into hers. 'Hands off! Come on Jenny, back to the old homestead.'

When they once more reached Embury Court, Gerry stood hesitating in front of the door to the Collins' quarters. He seemed reluctant to join Leila and the Mountfields on the terrace.

'Come in and have a cuppa with us,' Jenny suggested at last when he made no move to depart.

Gerry accepted with surprising alacrity, and Aunt Sarah was, of course, delighted to ply the young master with tea and biscuits.

'So it was you in that helicopter which flew over this morning,' she said. 'It caused quite an excitement.'

'It was a big thrill for us too,' said Jenny. 'It was wonderful experience.'

'Yes,' agreed Gerry. 'You don't realize what a splendid place Embury is until you see it from the air.'

'You are a very fortunate young man to have such an inheritance,' Aunt Sarah burbled on. 'You must take care of it.'

'I know,' sighed Gerry, unusually

serious, 'but it's a burden as well as a blessing. It takes a lot of upkeep, and I never did like responsibility.'

'You'll have to find a wife who shares your love of the old place,' cooed Aunt Sarah.

'You sound just like my parents,' grinned Gerry.

Jenny flushed. Aunt Sarah really was impossible.

'We had a splendid lunch at the Aero Club,' she interposed hastily.

But Aunt Sarah was not to be deterred.

'We have done good business with the tourists this season,' she persisted. 'Jenny has been a big success with them. She has such a lot of talent.'

'I know,' agreed Gerry smiling across at the blushing Jenny. 'She's a gem.'

As soon as he decently could Gerry got to his feet.

'It's a lovely evening,' he said. 'Care to come for a short stroll round the grounds, Jenny?'

Blushing even more deeply, Jenny,

joined him by the door.

'Yes, I'd enjoy that,' she said.

'Thank you Mrs Dixon for a very enjoyable tea-time,' Gerry said politely and taking Jenny's hand drew her out into the garden.

They strolled happily hand in hand across the courtyard and through the archway into the shadows of the pleached alley. There Gerry took her into his arms.

'You're the loveliest creature I've ever seen,' he said, kissing her hungrily. 'It's been a perfectly wonderful day,' he mumbled into her hair.

Despite her best intentions, Jenny felt herself go limp in his arms and she yielded to his caresses. 'I love you, Jenny,' he said.

'And I love you, Gerry,' she heard herself saying.

When at last, glowing and dishevelled she returned to the house, Aunt Sarah eyed her with a knowing smile.

'Did you have a nice walk, dear?' she asked archly.

'Yes, very pleasant, thank you, Aunt,' answered Jenny, trying to look prim.

Aunt Sarah smiled to herself. Her intuition had been right from the beginning. It had never failed her yet.

The little family in the West Wing went to bed happy that evening. All was going to plan and they were sure of a splendid future.

9

The next day was hotter than ever. It seemed that this summer would never end. Jenny waited happily for Gerry to seek her out and whisk her away to the Country Club swimming-pool again. But he did not appear.

'Where is Gerry today?' enquired Aunt Sarah.

'He's busy,' snapped Jenny in reply, not wishing to confess that she had no idea what he was up to.

Giving up hope, she wandered off into the gardens. Guided by the refreshing sound of tinkling water she sought out the snake fountain and stood beneath its cooling spray. After the past week's excitements life felt very flat. The splashing of the fountain revived her spirits and she began to wonder what had happened to Alan while she had been enjoying high jinks with Gerry. She found him in his studio hard at work over his portrait of Leila.

'Hullo!' he said. 'Where's Gerry?'

'How should I know?' snapped Jenny. 'I wish people wouldn't keep asking me that. I'm not his keeper.'

'Sorry!' said Alan, stepping back from his easel and surveying his work with his head on one side. 'What do you think of it so far?'

Jenny moved over to his side to give the portrait her full attention. It was a study of the eternal female which lurks in every woman. Alan had emphasized his sitter's green eyes so that they glowed in contrast to her black velvet gown. They seemed to follow the spectator like the eyes of the Mona Lisa.

'The cat!' exclaimed Jenny.

'Exactly!' smiled Alan gratified. 'I think I've caught her personality remarkably well.'

'What does she think of it?'

'She's delighted. I've given her just the dangerous untamed character she

156

wanted to convey.'

'I see. So you got on with her remarkably well, too?'

'Like life-long buddies. She's got a pretty wit.'

'I never noticed it. What's she witty about?'

'High society.'

'Huh! I hate witty people. They're so clever at other people's expense.'

'It's a defence mechanism. They feel threatened.'

'Rubbish! Whatever has Leila got to feel threatened about?'

'Other younger cats, clawing their way up. It's the law of the jungle.'

Jenny shuddered.

'How very unpleasant,' she remarked with a superior air. 'I don't know how you put up with her.'

Alan laughed in an infuriatingly masculine way.

'Women are a constant source of amusement to me,' he said. 'That's why I like painting them.'

'Then I'll leave you to enjoy the joke,'

spat Jenny, and walked out on him.

She was glad that she had a tour to guide that afternoon for Aunt Sarah was still worrying at the question of Gerry's whereabouts. This became her aunt's constant refrain for several days, becoming ever more urgent when Gerry failed to appear.

'He's busy studying,' Jenny improvised in an attempt to silence her.

'Oh, did he phone you?' asked Sarah.

'Yes,' Jenny lied, 'he — he had to go up to Cambridge to read at the Fitzwilliam.'

As the days passed, she strove to convince herself that this was the true explanation of Gerry's desertion. She even, much to her own shame, sneaked round to the private car-park to see if his car was still in its usual place.

'Perhaps he's ill — in hospital!' thought Jenny wildly. 'Perhaps I ought to ring him. No! I'll not lower myself that far. He could have sent a message, even if he were dying.' Her heart turned over at the thought. He might have had an accident, fallen down stairs or something. But Uncle Henry would surely have heard about that. No, Gerry had gone up to London by train. That was it. He was studying at the British Library or the Inns of Court or somewhere.

Alas, her comforting fantasy was soon to be shattered. The next day Lord Mountfields summoned all his staff to gather on the terrace to hear an announcement.

Now there was another question for Aunt Sarah to puzzle over.

'Hasn't he told you anything?' she badgered Uncle Henry. 'You're his right-hand man aren't you? What are you hiding?'

'I assure you I have no idea what it's all about,' reiterated Henry.

'Lord Mountfields is probably selling out to the Japanese,' suggested Jenny.

'Don't say that!' shuddered Aunt Sarah. 'That would be terrible.'

'It's not at all likely,' soothed Uncle

Henry. 'We'll all find out tomorrow, doubtless.'

'Well I think he should have told you at least,' grumbled Aunt Sarah. 'Perhaps this is why we haven't seen Gerry. Perhaps his father has got him involved in some unnecessary innovation or something unpleasant.'

She was soon to discover that the truth was even more unpleasant than she had imagined.

Dutifully they all gathered on the terrace at the appointed time, amid a babble of questions and wild conjectures. However when Lord and Lady Mountfields, Gerry and Leila emerged from the french windows all smiles, fears fled away. The announcement was going to be a happy one.

Lord Mountfields stretched out his arm to Gerry and Leila and motioned them forward. Beaming with satisfaction he made the promised proclamation.

'My wife and I have great pleasure in announcing that a marriage has been arranged between my son and heir, the

Honourable Gerald, and Miss Leila Barton. I am sure you will all join with me in wishing them well.'

A chorus of agreement followed and Uncle Henry in his capacity of Chief Curator, stepped forward and shook hands with Gerry and planted a discreet kiss on Leila's cheek. He was delighted, he told the newly affianced couple, to wish them every happiness on behalf of his staff. He was followed by the butler who added his congratulations on behalf of the domestics. Then the head gardener insisted on taking his turn in the limelight. He pushed forward his little daughter who presented Leila with a hastily arranged bouquet of roses. Following the child strode Alan, beaming with delight, to offer his heartfelt congratulations. He kissed Leila lovingly and pumped Gerry's hand.

'Wonderful news old boy,' he said.

Unfortunately the effect of this *bonhomie* was spoilt by the fact that he was still clothed in his paint-spattered livery.

Throughout all this joyous rigmarole Jenny and Aunt Sarah stood silent, sickly smiles pinned to their faces. Aunt Sarah had flushed scarlet, but Jenny had turned white.

'Well!' burst out Aunt Sarah once they had regained the sanctuary of their own quarters. 'I've never been so disappointed in a man in all my life!'

'Why's that?' asked Jenny, pretending unconcern.

'Such — such duplicity!' spluttered Aunt Sarah. 'I could have sworn he was seriously interested in you.'

'So could I,' thought Jenny inwardly while managing a light laugh.

'I told you we were just friends,' she snapped.

'This is excellent news,' declared Uncle Henry, coming in smiling. 'We were all hoping for this. Leila's money is just what the old place needs. There's so much to be done. The roof alone needs thousands.'

'Really Henry! What a mercenary way to look at an engagement. It's supposed to be love, not a commercial transaction.'

'They're well suited,' Henry defended himself.

'Huh! Then why has he been hanging round Jenny these past weeks?'

'We were just friends,' repeated Jenny wearily. 'Well I can't stay chatting here. There's something I want to look up in the library ready for this afternoon.'

Hastily Jenny made her escape to the library. She got down a large tome and opened it at random. She sat down in front of it and stared at it blindly. She was trembling with shock. She had never guessed at anything like Gerry's sudden engagement, despite Leila's warning.

'So she's won, has she, the witch!' she muttered. 'Well I wish her joy. She's bought him quite blatantly! It will be a peculiar marriage.' Her face burned at the memory of Gerry's passionate kisses, and she shuddered at the thought of the way she had returned them. He had said he loved her, the lying swine! And, most shameful of all, she had said she loved him! How could she have been such a fool! Leila was right, she was nothing but a silly old-fashioned schoolmarm to be swept off her feet by a kiss. Tears welled up in her eyes at the memory. She crushed them down savagely. No! She would not cry for such a worthless wimp. Never! He had just done what his daddy told him. The worm!

Savage anger rose up within her, rescuing her from her shame. Alan had warned her against Gerry, told her that he was nothing but a two-timing cad. Somehow that made her no fonder of Alan. How dared he follow her round with his lecherous curiosity! He probably knew that Gerry was a playboy because he was one himself.

'It takes one to know one,' she fumed.

She hated all men, they were worthless, all of them. She slammed the book shut and jumped up. Well, that was it. She couldn't get her revenge on Gerry without lowering herself further, so she'd take the stuffing out of Alan.

She found him in his studio, putting the finishing touches to his portrait of Leila, and whistling happily.

'Wonderful news, isn't it?' he greeted her.

'Is it?'

'Of course! Couldn't be better from my point of view. Once the engagement is announced in the papers, everyone will be queuing to see my portrait. Superb publicity!'

'Is that all you care about?'

'Not quite all. I'm overjoyed for dear Gerry. The lovely Leila and all that money. That's him nicely settled.'

'She's bought him!'

'She's bought Embury. That's worth far more than sweet little Gerry.'

'That makes it worse than ever. It's all quite horrible.'

'Nonsense, she'll make a splendid chatelaine.'

'But what about Gerry?'

'He's only incidental to the arrangement. But don't worry. I expect she'll keep him on a long lead.'

'Oh, I'm not worrying about him. He's dug his own grave.'

'And a pretty plush-lined grave it is.'

'You've got no heart, no decent feelings. All you care about is your wretched paint.'

'And to what purer goddess could a man dedicate his soul?'

'Pure! Huh! Is that why you go about dressed in filthy rags?'

'My lovely goddess likes me like that. It proves I'm all hers.'

'Well I don't like it. You might have put on a clean shirt for this afternoon.'

'I haven't got one. Would you care to wash one out for me, since you're so anxious about my appearance?'

'No I wouldn't, you lazy hound! I couldn't care less about your appearance. Oh, stop whistling do, it's getting on my nerves.'

'How about a cup of tea and a doughnut? I've bought some fresh ones.'

'I hope they choke you. Goodbye!'

Jenny felt no better after this encounter. In fact she felt worse. It was not Alan's fault that Gerry had played her false. Not that Alan cared two hoots anyway. He was intolerably smug! She was glad she had a tour to conduct that afternoon. She hoped that would jerk her back to normality.

Unfortunately news of the engagement had leaked out, and the American matrons bombarded her with questions as to the beauty of the bride, the date and place of the wedding, and the well-hidden secret of the romance.

'I assure you, I know nothing,' she explained again and again. 'It was just as much a surprise to me as anyone.'

At long last the hateful day was over and Jenny was free to crawl up to bed. It was then, as she lay there alone in the silence, that she could no longer control the tears. She put her head under the duvet and sobbed with mingled disappointment and humiliation.

The next day was just as hot but

overcast. A pall blotted out the sun. There was not a breath of wind and not a leaf stirred. Thunder grumbled in the distance and the electricity in the air jangled through Jenny's head.

Aunt Sarah was dismayed at her haggard appearance.

'Do cheer up dear,' she cajoled. 'That young man wasn't worth upsetting yourself over.'

'I'm not in the least upset,' declared Jenny bravely. 'It's the weather that's getting me down. Thunder always makes me feel ill.'

Aunt Sarah pursed her lips disbelievingly but wisely said no more.

That evening a civic reception had been arranged at which it was planned to announce Gerry's engagement. Aunt Sarah and Uncle Henry had been commanded to attend in their official capacity.

'I'm afraid we can't possibly get out of it,' worried Aunt Sarah. 'We shall have to go and look delighted or they'll guess our annoyance.'

'But I *am* delighted,' protested Uncle Henry.

'For all the wrong reasons,' retorted his wife. 'I do hope you'll be all right Jenny, left on your own.'

'But I shan't be alone,' protested Jenny.

'I'm afraid that you will. Lord Mountfields has laid on a special celebration for the staff in the village hall. So the house will be deserted.'

'Of course I'll be all right!' replied Jenny, forcing a laugh. 'You are absurd, Aunt! I'm not a child any longer you know.'

'I don't know so much about that,' grumbled her aunt. 'You behave in a very childish way sometimes.'

'Anyway, Alan will be here I expect,' Jenny endeavoured to soothe her.

'Huh! I doubt if he'd be much use in an emergency.'

'There won't be any emergency,' Jenny reassured her. 'Now do stop worrying for heaven's sake! Relax! You look charming in that black satin gown.

It's just right. Mind you, don't outshine the bride-to-be.'

'Oh don't be so foolish, Jenny,' chided Aunt Sarah, preening herself in the mirror.

'I expect there'll be heaps of luscious food and quarts of champagne. I'll be in bed when you get back. Mind you, don't wake me singing.'

At last Henry succeeded in getting his clucking wife into the car and they disappeared down the drive.

Jenny sank back on the sofa with a book she had been intending to read all that holiday. But tonight it failed to hold her attention. Darkness had done nothing to cool the atmosphere, in fact it seemed hotter and more breathless than ever. Thunder growled in the distance like a wild animal waiting to pounce. She switched on the television, but the air was so full of atmospherics that it offered no entertainment.

Jenny sat in silence for a while, listening to the strange murmurings and rustlings which filled the house.

The ancient building too was restless, as though woken from its sleep by the approach of danger. Jenny could have sworn she heard footsteps down the long gallery and muffled groans.

She jumped up and shook herself firmly.

'Oh don't be so daft,' she told herself. 'It's the electricity in the air affecting the old oak in the wainscot.' She poured herself a long drink of lemonade and added ice to it, swirling it round in the glass so that its tinkling music drowned the travail of the house. She decided to go to bed and try to sleep. But she would not weep over Gerry's faithlessness again. Never! Not if she were stretched on the rack and tortured. The thought of the rack combined with all the ghostly noises of the house made her shudder. She ran up the winding stair to her bedroom fast, trying to escape from the manifold miseries of life.

It seemed hotter still in her room. She flung open the window and leaned out, attempting to cool her face. Across the dark courtyard a light gleamed from the Priest's House. Alan was restless too. Her heart softened towards him. He had warned her against Gerry. He must have known the way she had been cavorting with the lecher. He had every right to say 'I told you so'. But he had nobly kept silent. In fact he had done his best to cheer her up. She wished she had not been so nasty to him. It was not his fault that she had been such a fool.

Suddenly she made up her mind. She ran down the stairs and out into the darkness. The thunderstorm was nearer now. Quickly she flitted across the shadowed courtyard like a moth towards the light.

10

Alan was sitting on a folding chair outside the cottage, contemplating the darkness.

'Hullo!' he greeted her. 'Are you restless too?'

'Yes, and so is the house. Everyone's out and the emptiness is uncanny. I keep hearing footsteps.'

'Then sit here and keep me company,' he said, getting to his feet. 'I'll fetch another chair.'

'Do you believe in ghosts?' Jenny asked, when they were both comfortably settled.

'Of course I do. Don't you?'

'I do not.'

'They mean no harm. There are bound to be echoes of the past in such an old building. It must have weathered many an upheaval. So many memories of human joys and sorrows must have soaked into its walls.'

Jenny nodded in agreement. And they sat on in companionable silence for a while listening to the thunder growing ever closer, and watching the lightning illuminating the sky.

'Have you any family?' Jenny ventured to ask, sensing his loneliness.

'My parents are both flourishing but they're living in New Zealand with my sister's family,' he answered.

'How about you?'

'My father's dead,' said Jenny, 'and I've no brothers or sisters. I live alone with my mother.'

He stretched out his hand and squeezed hers in sympathy.

'So we're both orphans of the storm,' he smiled.

'And what a storm!' said Jenny, as an even brighter flash of lightning accompanied by a long menacing growl of thunder lit the façade of the house in an eerie white light.

'I'd like to try and paint that,' said

Alan. 'But it would take a Turner to do it justice.'

The thunder growled again in response to his appreciative words, as if to show him what further wonders it had in store.

Even as he spoke the heavens split open with an almighty roar, and a forked tongue of lightning streaked out like the cruel breath of a dragon and licked round the ancient roof of the mansion. A menacing sheet of red flame curled round the chimneys, and two windows in the façade glowed crimson as the fire took hold.

'Alan, the house is on fire!' cried Jenny, clutching his arm. 'It's the writing room!'

'Oh my God! The Donalettos!' cried Alan leaping to his feet. 'Get the fire brigade quickly. And stay there. Don't follow me.'

He ran out into the fitful glare and disappeared through the postern door into the house.

Jenny flung herself into the cottage,

overturning her chair in her haste. She snatched up the phone and dialled 999. Her frantic tones alerted the operator to the urgency of her call.

'The fire brigade will be along in a few minutes,' he soothed. 'Now keep calm and stay out of danger.'

But Jenny did not obey. She sped out of the cottage and followed Alan into the house. She met him coming down the stairs, three of the precious paintings clasped to his chest. He thrust them into her arms.

'Take them out quickly and stay out,' he ordered and turned to go back into the furnace.

Jenny ran across the courtyard with the pictures and stacked them carefully against the wall of the studio. But she could not stay in safety while Alan was in danger. She dashed back into the house and up the stairs calling desperately, 'Alan! Come out quickly!' The roar of the flames drowned her voice.

She fought her way through the

smoke-filled drawing-room to the door-way of the writing-room. The little room was now ablaze.

'Alan!' she shrieked. 'Alan! Where are you?'

His blackened figure approached, clasping the last of the Donalettos.

'You little fool!' he coughed. 'I told you to keep out.' He shoved her violently back through the doorway. She fell, striking her head on the doorjamb and lay still.

'Dear God, the ceiling,' gasped Alan and threw himself on top of her body just as the ceiling came down with a terrifying roar. A piece of burning rafter fell across his legs. With superhuman effort he kicked the charred wood aside and got to his feet. He flung Jenny across his shoulder in a fireman's lift. Then with the picture under his other arm, he struggled down the stairs and out into the courtyard, collapsing in a heap on the stones.

As they lay there, the wind rose and the thunder yielded to the rain, which lashed down savagely as though it meant to drown all living creatures. The fire fought back but could not withstand it. The hideous glow of the flames was subdued.

The cold deluge on her face revived Jenny. She sat up and peered about her.

'Alan,' she mumbled, putting out her hand to find him. 'Alan.'

'It's all right, Jenny,' he whispered, fighting to keep the pain from his voice. 'We're safe now.'

They lay there coughing and spluttering to clear the smoke from their lungs. It seemed an age before the fire engines came screaming up the drive, led by a police car and followed by an ambulance. A police officer leapt from his car and shouted into the darkness. 'Two casualties here! Stretched needed.' The ambulance men ran up with a stretcher and bent over Alan.

'I'm all right, see to the girl first,' he croaked.

They took no notice of his protests,

but lifted him gently on to the stretcher and carried him to the ambulance. A policeman helped Jenny to her feet and, with an arm round her shoulders, persuaded her to follow.

'There's nothing wrong with me,' she protested. 'Leave me and see to Alan.'

'Get in Miss,' ordered the officer. 'Come along now.'

'Get in Jenny,' Alan called weakly.

Meekly she obeyed, and crouched down by his side. Tears were running down her blackened face, making little rivulets down her cheeks.

'I'm sorry,' she sobbed. 'It's all my fault.'

He reached out and clutched her hand.

'Rubbish!' he choked. 'Together we saved the paintings.'

'Don't try to talk,' commanded the ambulance officer, placing an oxygen mask over Alan's face.

When they arrived at the hospital, nurses ran out to attend to Alan. His stretcher was wheeled away down an echoing corridor into the depths of the building. Jenny was not allowed to follow him, but was led into the casualty department. Her teeth were chattering and she could not still her trembling.

'Sit down dear,' said a nurse kindly. 'Have you any burns?'

Dumbly Jenny held out her hands.

'We'll soon put those right,' encouraged the nurse. 'You were lucky.'

'Alan?' Jenny managed to gasp.

'Is he your boyfriend dear? Don't worry about him. He's in the best of hands.'

She wrapped a blanket round Jenny and efficiently set to work on her burns. But in spite of encouragement Jenny continued to shiver and shake.

'Shock,' pronounced the doctor when at last he arrived.

He drew the nurse aside and Jenny heard the words 'sedative' and 'bed rest'.

'Yes, Doctor, of course,' said the nurse.

Jenny was led she knew not where, undressed, draped in a hospital gown and put to bed. Another nurse approached with a syringe and jabbed it into her arm. Jenny sighed and lack back.

'That's right, have a little sleep, you'll soon feel better,' said somebody.

Jenny closed her eyes and slept for a while. The curtain was drawn round her bed to protect her from the prying eyes of the other patients, who were all agog to know the worst.

'Show's over!' snapped the ward sister, dropping her soothing tones.

'Go back to sleep all of you. It's the middle of the night.'

All was quiet in the ward, or at least as quiet as it ever is in a hospital. Jenny gradually slipped away into a grey mist as the sedative did its work.

She awoke to the clatter of the hospital beginning the day. Her trembling had ceased but she felt as though she were recovering from a long illness. The curtain round her bed was pulled back and an orderly stood over her with a cup of tea.

'What? Why?' she spluttered.

'Drink this dear,' said the orderly. 'You've been in a fire.'

Fire! The dreadful word brought all the horror of the evening flooding back. Once again the flames roared round her head and the acrid smoke filled her nostrils. She tried to scream but only a croaking sound came from her lips.

A nurse, seeing her agitation, bustled up.

'Swallow these dear,' she commanded handing her a couple of sinister-looking pills and a glass of water. Jenny choked them down obediently and the roaring of the flames receded.

'It's all over now dear,' soothed the orderly. 'You're quite safe here. Doctor will be along soon.'

When the doctor came Jenny was beginning to feel more human.

'How is Alan — Mr Freeman?' she asked.

'He's a strong young man, he'll live,'

said the doctor. 'Now you concentrate on getting yourself well and leave Mr. Freeman to us. Another day and night here for this young lady,' he added to the nurse, and turned away to deal with another patient.

But Jenny was not pacified. As soon as she judged the doctor was well away, she nipped out of bed, wrapped the voluminous hospital gown around her and tiptoed out of the ward. She found the corridor down which Alan had been carried and crept along it. At last, after peering in vain into many cubicles, she found him.

Her heart turned over when she saw him. He lay there, his eyes shut, his legs propped up on a cradle. His face was drawn and white and his jaunty mask had fallen from him. Jenny longed to take him in her arms and comfort him as she would a suffering child. She tiptoed over to him and put her hand gently on his shoulder.

'Alan,' she whispered.

He opened his eyes and gathered his

strength into a smile.

'I'm fine,' he answered, 'couldn't be better. How are you?'

'Just fine,' said Jenny and bent down and gently kissed his forehead.

Then, seeing a nurse advancing menacingly, she sped back to her own ward and scrambled into bed. Once more the tears were streaming down her face. She lay there trembling and struggling to suppress her sobs. A neighbouring patient, seeing her distress, pressed the bell for the nurse. She bustled up, clucking disapprovingly.

'This won't do at all,' she said. 'All your troubles are over now. There's nothing to fear.'

She quickly fetched another evil-looking potion and held it out.

'Drink this,' she said. 'It will make you feel better.'

Jenny swallowed it down obediently and merciful sleep overcame her.

The next morning she felt better. The flames in her head had died down and she was ready to face life again. After the doctor had examined her hands and pronounced them to be 'doing fine' she was told to get up.

'You're lucky to be such a healthy young woman,' he said. 'Keep out of burning buildings in future.'

'Oh I will!' promised Jenny. 'Never again!'

'Your aunt's here,' an attendant told her. 'She's waiting for you in the lobby. She's brought you these clean clothes.'

'Good old Aunt Sarah!' thought Jenny, pulling them on gratefully.

She turned to the nurse who had tended her during those two nightmare days and nights.

'Thank you for looking after me,' she said.

'It's a pleasure when a patient responds as well as you have done,' smiled the nurse. 'Now off you go and forget all about it.'

Thus dismissed, Jenny walked some-what shakily out of the ward. But she did not go to the lobby where Aunt Sarah awaited her; instead she turned down the corridor which led to Alan. How could she forget about it while Alan still lay in his bed, so pale and silent?

'I can't go without saying goodbye to him,' she thought.

Alan too seemed better. He was sitting propped up on his pillows a sketch-book in his hand.

'I've come to say goodbye,' she said. 'They're sending me out today.'

'That's good,' he answered. 'You certainly look better than yesterday.'

Jenny flushed.

'I didn't think you noticed me yesterday,' she said.

'Of course I noticed you. I notice everything. It's my job.' He smiled up at her with his old jaunty grin.

'Don't worry about me,' he told her. 'I'm as tough as old boots. I'll be out of here soon. I've got to be. I've got an exhibition to arrange.'

'Then I'll say goodbye,' she said hesitantly, hoping he would contradict her.

'Not goodbye but *au revoir,*' he answered. 'I'll see you at the Exton Galleries. You'll come won't you?'

'Of course I'll come.'

'Then I'll let you know the date. Cheer up. We're neither of us dead yet. I don't intend to be. I've got work to do.'

'So have I for that matter. You're not the only dedicated professional.'

'Hurrah! That's the spirit. Give me a kiss to wish me luck.'

Jenny bent and kissed his cheek.

'Cheerio,' she said, pretending not to care.

A male attendant approached with an air of importance.

'Your aunt's here,' he said. 'She's waiting in the hall and getting agitated.'

Jenny turned away and walked out of the ward.

'See you at the Exton Galleries,' Alan called after her.

Jenny bit back the tears, determined not to cry again.

Alan was a brute. All he thought

about was his beastly paintings. Well, she didn't care. She had work to do herself.

Aunt Sarah was indeed agitated. She folded Jenny in her arms.

'How are you darling? she cried. 'Your mother is in such a state. You must phone her as soon as we get back to Embury.'

'I shall have to go home myself soon,' said Jenny. 'I've only got a few days' holiday left.'

'We'll see about that,' answered Aunt Sarah grimly. 'Come along darling. I'm in charge of you now.'

Jenny foresaw a tussle ahead but for the moment she was content to sit back in the car and be carried to Embury.

She was relieved to find that the damage was not so extensive as she had feared.

'The rain came just in time to save the Drawing-Room,' said Uncle Henry. 'Only the study is seriously damaged. We're working hard to restore it and you saved the Donalettos.'

'How are they?' she asked.

'Untouched thanks to your heroism.'

'It was Alan who saved them, not me.'

'It was very foolish of you both. Treasures though the paintings are, they're not worth the price of life.'

'Alan wouldn't agree with that.'

'I've had to revise my opinion of that young man,' admitted Aunt Sarah.

'He's a hero!' said Jenny hotly.

'Maybe, but he should not have allowed you to run into danger.'

Jenny laughed.

'He couldn't stop me,' she said.

'You always were a disobedient child,' said Aunt Sarah.

Scarcely had she had time to settle once again into Embury ways, when the heir apparent arrived to thank her.

'You're a truly wonderful girl,' Gerry said admiringly. 'You must let me kiss you to show you how grateful I am.'

Jenny coldly proffered her cheek for

189

his salute. She was surprised to find that he now meant nothing to her. She could not imagine what she had seen in him. How could she have thought him the answer to her girlish dreams? She felt a thousand years older than the careless girl who had flirted with Gerry in the sunshine and wept at his betrayal.

Gerry was a wimp and Alan was a brute, she told herself. She was finished with men. She would henceforth dedicate her life to her work and become a headmistress, and after that an inspector. She'd swan around the schools, criticizing and putting the fear of God into all and sundry. She'd be a regular right-down bitch.

She laughed aloud at her thoughts, startling Aunt Sarah.

'What are you laughing at?' she enquired.

'I was thinking it will be nice to get back to work and see my colleagues and all those naughty children again.'

'Are you sure you feel up to it? You look very pale.'

'Of course I am! There's nothing wrong with me.'

'But how are you going to travel?'

'Drive of course.'

'Nonsense. You're not going to drive after the ordeal you've been through. Henry will drive your car and come back on the train.'

'I'm afraid I can't do that,' said Henry. 'I can't leave my post with all the repairs to supervise.'

'Oh very well, then I'll drive her, and you can meet me at the station. I suppose you can manage that.'

'Very well, dear,' answered Henry meekly.

'Good. That's arranged then,' said Aunt Sarah decisively.

'It's really not necessary,' protested Jenny.

'You must let me be the judge of that,' stated Aunt Sarah in her best 'steam-roller' voice. 'I shall enjoy seeing your mother again. We've got a lot of gossip to catch up on.'

'I'll bet you have,' thought Jenny resignedly.

She hugged Uncle Henry in sympathy.

'I've had the holiday of a lifetime,' she said.

11

Mrs Collins welcomed the travellers with open arms and anxious enquiries.

'That dreadful fire!' she fussed. 'I've been so worried.'

'There was really no need, mother,' soothed Jenny. 'I'm absolutely fine.'

After a while she left the two sisters to exchange confidences in private.

'I'll go and unpack,' she said. 'And I've got to get ready for school on Monday.'

Early next morning Sarah insisted that she must return to Embury.

'I must get back and see what Henry's up to,' she said.

'Whatever could he be up to?' laughed Jenny.

'Oh, you never know with men,' said her aunt. 'You daren't take your eyes off them.'

Jenny drove her to the station and kissed her goodbye.

'Thanks, Aunt Sarah,' she said.

'Whatever for?'

'For not telling mother about my silly escapade with Gerry.'

'I've forgotten all about it,' said Sarah. 'And I advise you to do the same.'

'I'm going to do just that,' resolved Jenny.

As she watched her aunt's train rumble out of the station and disappear round a bend in the track, she hoped that all memories of the past hot summer would dissolve into a dream. But they obstinately refused to fade. Rather it was the world of home and school which seemed unreal.

On her first day of term her colleagues crowded round her to hear the tale of her adventures. They were particularly eager to hear about the Honourable Gerald and her romance with him.

'We saw the pictures of you dancing

with him,' they informed her. 'The newspapers all dubbed you his latest flame.'

'What rot!' scoffed Jenny. 'It was just a holiday flirtation. You know how these things are.'

'No we don't!' they chorused. 'We've no idea. Come on, tell us. We want to know what goes on in these exalted circles.'

'Nothing much goes on at all,' said Jenny. 'Just a few outings. Nothing serious. The gossip writers always make mountains out of molehills.'

'There's no smoke without fire,' teased Norah. She was feeling particularly cheerful, for her friendship with Tim had progressed under the clear skies of Greece.

'You're all being very stupid. Come down to earth, do,' pleaded Jenny. 'He's engaged to Leila Barton.'

'Yes we read about that too,' her inquisitors continued. 'Were you devastated?'

'Not in the least. I knew all about it

long before it was announced,' lied Jenny.

To her relief the interest in her so-called romance soon died down, and school politics took over the talk in the staff-room. Jenny did her best to interest herself in the discussion of the new curriculum and the pros and cons of putting seven-year-olds to the test. Unfortunately these professional questions seemed very flat and dreary. She could not prevent her thoughts straying to Alan and his forthcoming exhibition.

Under the pretext of asking about the progress of the repairs at Embury, Jenny rang up her aunt.

'Seen anything of Alan?' she enquired carelessly, when the tale of the lazy workmen had been told.

'Oh yes, he came down last week to fetch his precious paintings,' said her aunt.

'How did he seem?'

'All right I suppose. You could never call that young man normal, could you? I had to have a word with him about the state he'd left the Priest's House in, but I doubt if he was listening. What he needs is a wife.'

'Who'd take him on?'

'No woman in her right mind,' decided Aunt Sarah. 'He'd need a very firm hand and be hardly worth the bother.'

This little homily from her aunt did nothing to cheer Jenny. She had learnt that Alan had recovered from his ordeal in the fire, but he was obviously not thinking of her.

A few weeks later another reminder of the summer arrived on the doormat, in the shape of an imposing invitation to Gerry's and Leila's wedding at St. Mary's, Cadogan Square and afterwards at the Beaumont Hotel. The card sported a deckled edge and was decorated with silver bells.

Aunt Sarah had swallowed her disappointment at her failure to capture Gerald for Jenny, and had decided to extract all the enjoyment she could from this grand occasion.

'Perhaps it's just as well nothing came of Jenny's romance with Gerald,' she told her husband. 'She would have been displayed as a poor beggar-maid in the Mountfields' circles.'

'Just as well, my dear,' responded Henry, wisely refraining from adding 'I told you so'.

'I must ring up Frances at once and ask if Jenny's had an invitation,' Sarah continued, anxious for another delightful gossip. The telephone line hummed between Northcote and Embury. Lord Mountfields was laying on a coach to take his staff to London, and the curator and his wife had an honoured place upon it. Since Jenny's invitation included a guest, she invited her mother to accompany her so that she should not be left out of the excitement.

Jenny had a private reason to feel a tremor of anticipation. Alan would, of course, have been invited also. Surely he would be there. In this hope she dressed herself with the utmost care, and was pleased when her mother commended her appearance.

On the appointed day Jenny and her mother arrived early and were led to a place of vantage on the bridegroom's side of the church. St. Mary's was a solid nineteenth-century building with somewhat garish Victorian stained glass. It was a favourite place for fashionable weddings because its wide aisle leading up to the altar gave the bridal procession a magnificent opportunity for display. Today every sturdy pillar was festooned with carnations in rainbow colours, interwoven with variegated ivy. The altar and communion rail were adorned with pure white lilies and maiden hair fern.

'No expense spared,' whispered Jenny's mother as they sat trying to look dignified.

'There's plenty where that came from. Barton's Supermarkets!' Jenny hissed.

Gerry and his best man, both impeccably tailored, were fidgetting somewhat nervously in the front pew, seemingly not knowing what to do with their top-hats.

'Gerald's very handsome, isn't he?' whispered Jenny's mother. 'A real heart-throb.'

'Is he?' answered Jenny. 'He doesn't appeal to me.'

She found it impossible to sit still. She turned her head hopefully to inspect every new arrival, but, alas, Alan was not one of them. When at last the organ pealed out the joyful news that the bride had arrived, Jenny rose to her feet with a heavy heart.

Leila had chosen a Regency theme for her bridal procession. The high-waisted, flowing style suited her elegant figure. Her gown was of white silk and her veil was fastened by a crown of pale pink rose-buds. She held a bouquet of the same delicate flowers which cascaded down the folds of her gown. She glided down the aisle on her father's arm looking the very picture of sweet purity. She was followed by four little girls in similar array. She had wisely avoided having small boys in her retinue, lest their antics should distract attention from herself. Led by a full choir in red cassocks and lacy surplices she proceeded slowly to the altar rails, where Gerry awaited her. The officiating cleric, an imposing figure in a flowing white surplice who was obviously a candidate for a bishopric, greeted this enchanting couple with a benign smile, and commenced the service in a rich baritone.

'Dearly beloved,' he intoned.

To Jenny the actors in this age-old ritual seemed unreal, like characters in a film.

When the couple was safely united the guests were whisked away from a barrage of photographers in a fleet of limousines to the Beaumont Hotel, where more luxury awaited them. This hostelry was one of the few left in London still furnished in lush Edwardian style. The carpets were inches thick, the long curtains were of plush brown velvet and crystal chandeliers dripped from the ceilings.

Jenny's mother and aunt gravitated towards one another, eager to exchange notes.

'Too much of everything, I thought,' commented Jenny's mother.

'Almost vulgar,' agreed Sarah. 'I'm sure Lady Mountfields can't have approved.'

'It could have done without the rosebuds,' added her sister. 'Orange blossom is much more bridal.'

'And far more fitting,' nodded Sarah.

'It shall make it my business to see that you have something much much simpler and more youthful for your wedding Jenny,' said her mother.

'I'm never going to have a wedding,' stated Jenny firmly.

'Nonsense, of course you will!' contradicted her aunt. 'There are plenty of fish in the sea.'

'But I don't want to marry a wet fish,' snapped Jenny.

'I wonder Alan Freeman isn't here,'

continued Sarah. 'He might have made some useful contacts.'

'He probably couldn't find a clean shirt,' said Jenny drearily.

'Huh!' exclaimed her aunt. 'I shall never understand that young man.'

Fortunately the champagne was vintage and did much to restore their flagging spirits.

Uncle Henry drank to the newly-weds enthusiastically.

'Now we shan't have to sell the Donalettos,' he murmured.

Jenny drained her glass and took another from the tray held out by a waitress. She needed sustenance.

★　★　★

Not long after her disappointment at Alan's absence Jenny sat alone in her classroom feeling very dismal. It was late afternoon and the school was quiet save for the distant clanking of a cleaner's bucket. She put her elbows on her desk and laid her head in her hands.

The amazing summer was definitely over. Winter had settled over the land and Jenny felt as grey as the skies. Her plan to concentrate on her profession was not proving a success. Tim, working late on his arrangements for the football season, discovered her there.

'Hullo! You look like a wet weekend in Manchester,' he said.

'I'm tired I suppose,' Jenny excused herself.

'That fire upset you more than you pretend,' said Tim sympathetically.

'Yes I think it did. I still have nightmares about it.'

'You need cheering up,' said Tim. 'Why not come down to the club this evening? There's a disco on.'

'What about Norah?'

'Oh, she's going to a Spanish class or something. I'm quite free. We're not engaged you know.'

'All right. You're on,' said Jenny. 'I could do with a night out.'

That evening Jenny tried hard to cast care aside and enjoy herself, but it was uphill work. She laughed and gyrated with the best, but her mirth had a hollow ring.

'I'm too old for this,' she told Tim. 'I can't get back into the swing of it.'

'I'll soon get you into the swing of it,' declared Tim, and seizing her arms he swung her round violently.

Jenny laughed and gasped for breath, but she was not really amused. Try to escape though she might, all her thoughts were concentrated on Alan and his promised exhibition. She was keyed up with the long wait for his summons.

Every evening she retired to her room with her radio to listen to 'Kaleido-scope's' review of the arts. She had almost given up hope when the miracle occurred.

'Alan Freeman, a brilliant newcomer to the art world,' said the cultured voice of the presenter.

Jenny leapt up and turned the radio up high so as not to miss a word.

'Norman Elder has spent the day at

Freeman's exhibition at the Exton Galleries,' continued the presenter. 'What did you think of his work, Norman?'

'I thought it quite brilliant,' enthused the critic. 'His portraits are remarkably vivid. He has a most unusual colour sense?'

'So you were impressed?'

'Yes I was. This young man is worth watching. His work reminded me of the early Picasso.'

'Oh, I wouldn't go as far as that,' put in a carping female voice.

'You wouldn't!' Jenny told her indignantly. 'What do you know about it, you silly old hag?'

'But I'd agree he's worth watching,' continued the female voice. 'His sketches from Embury Court were particularly attractive, I thought.'

'That's better. Carry on like that and we shan't quarrel,' Jenny told the empty air.

Her head whirled and felt it might burst with triumph. She jumped up and did a dance of delight around her bedroom.

In the middle of her dance the phone rang. She hurtled down the stairs and stood panting by the phone, anxious not to appear too eager.

'Answer that for me, will you dear,' her mother called from the sitting-room.

Jenny lifted the phone.

'Hullo,' she said.

'Oh hullo, Jenny,' answered a woman's voice. 'Is your mother available? I want a word.'

'It's Barbara,' called Jenny, trying to keep the disappointment out of her voice. 'She wants to speak to you.'

Jenny trailed into the sitting-room and sat fidgetting while her mother and Barbara gossiped interminably. She tapped her feet and twisted her fingers and muttered under her breath.

'Oh shut up both of you. Get off the line.'

Her mother had scarcely put the phone down when it rang again.

'It's for you dear,' she called. 'Some

young man or other. He sounds drunk to me.'

Jenny sped to the hall and took the receiver from her mother's hand.

'Jenny!' called Alan's voice. 'I've arrived!'

'I know. I've just been listening to Kaleidoscope.'

'I'm not dreaming am I? Tell me I'm not.'

'If you're dreaming then so am I.'

'Then let's not wake up, ever. 'Are you coming tomorrow?'

'Try and keep me away. It's Saturday so I'm quite free.'

'Right then, I'll meet you in the vestibule. Do you know the way?'

'I'll take a taxi. This is an occasion.'

'It certainly is. Two o'clock then outside the front entrance. Wear that blue frock.'

'Don't be daft. I'd be blue all over if I wore that in this weather.'

'Put four cardigans over the top, but you must wear that dress. I'm counting on it. Must say goodbye now. I'm surrounded by eager news-hounds. See you tomorrow without fail.'

Jenny skipped into the sitting-room.

'That was Alan,' she said. 'His exhibition's a success.'

Her mother smiled knowingly at her daughter's miraculous transformation.

'I should like to meet this amazing young man,' she said.

Jenny got out her blue summer dress and ironed it with extra care.

'You're not going to wear that?' commented her mother.

'Yes I must. Alan asked for it specially.'

'I'm beginning to agree with Sarah, the man's crazy.'

'No he's not,' retorted Jenny hotly. 'He's a genius.'

'Oh, I've never met one of those!' teased her mother.

Never had the fast train to Victoria crawled so slowly as that taking Jenny to meet Alan. She tried to do a crossword puzzle but could not even think of the word for 'female sheep' in three letters.

In the end she just wrote in anything. It helped her to pass the time.

However despite the apparent slowness of the train she arrived at the gallery on time.

Alan, looking unnaturally smart, was waiting, not in the vestibule but on the pavement outside. Jenny stepped out of her taxi into his arms.

'Jenny I've made it!' he said, and kissed her exuberantly.

'So you found a clean shirt,' she said.

Alan took her hand and led her proudly round his exhibition. Many of the pictures already bore the round, red sticker which meant they had been sold. Jenny, who only knew his work from the sketches he had made at Embury was astonished at the breadth of his vision. His vivid portraits of the various characters and nationalities to be seen in London were attracting a lot of attention. But the picture which drew all eyes was that of a girl in a blue summer dress standing by a stone statue. The other visitors quickly recognized Jenny as the *Girl in Blue Dress*.

'Why I do believe the reality is as pretty as the picture,' remarked a courteous old gentleman, smiling at Jenny's flushed face and shining eyes.

'It's the best picture in your show, young man,' said a dowager in an expensive mink coat. 'I'd like to buy it.'

'I'm afraid it's not for sale,' said Alan firmly.

'I'll pay you twice what you're asking.'

'I'm sorry, but no,' answered Alan. 'It's reserved.'

'Maybe madam would like to choose another canvas,' suggested Alan's agent hurrying to the rescue.

'Well, maybe,' agreed the dowager, consulting her catalogue. 'The Chinese with the hand-cart perhaps,' and she allowed herself to be led away.

'She's too late,' chuckled the old gentleman triumphantly. 'I've just bought that.'

Another focus of popular attention was the study in green-eyed feline grace which was the Honourable Leila Mountfields, the next Lady Mountfields in waiting.

'Fiendishly clever,' commented two young women who evidently knew Leila well. 'That's Leila to the life in all her cunning artfulness.'

'Careful! Don't say too much,' laughed her companion. 'She might stretch out her claws and scratch you.'

'Not for the first time,' responded her friend.

'You ought to have painted a portrait of Gerry too, to make a pair for the ancestral home,' said Jenny.

'I couldn't have done him justice,' answered Alan. 'I hated him so much I'd have given him horns and a tail.'

'He was quite harmless really,' laughed Jenny.

'No, harmless he was not!' said Alan grimly.

'Well he is now,' soothed Jenny. 'Leila

has him safely shackled.'

Jenny watched and listened with mounting excitement.

'This is wonderful, Alan,' she whispered. 'You're going to be a millionaire.'

'Not quite yet,' said Alan, 'but I'm on my way.'

12

When Jenny had seen and admired all the pictures, Alan took her into the little tea-room attached to the gallery. He led her to a little table in the window and ordered a pot of tea and a plate of doughnuts.

'I've got something to ask you,' he said, 'but I've come over all bashful.'

'That makes a change,' laughed Jenny. 'Come on then. Don't keep me in suspense.'

Jenny's heart was hammering and her head whirling. She bit off a large chunk of doughnut, hoping it would steady her.

'Well, here goes then,' said Alan, drawing a deep breath. 'Now I've arrived I've decided to get married.'

Jenny's heart turned over and she choked on the doughnut.

'But — but I thought you'd sworn off marriage!' she gasped.

'I've changed my mind,' said Alan.

'You see, I've fallen in love.'

Jenny turned cold and tears pricked at her eyes.

'Oh!' she exclaimed. 'You've kept that very secret.'

'It was secret once, but now it's in the open.'

'Then I hope you'll be very happy,' said Jenny bravely twisting her lips into a smile.

'I've not asked her yet. Do you think she'll accept me?'

'Of course she will, if she's got any sense,' said Jenny, revealing her true feelings to his shrewd gaze.

'You encourage me as always,' he grinned. 'So you think I'll make a good husband?'

'No you'll be a rotten one, but she'll accept you all the same,' choked Jenny, pretending that a piece of doughnut had got stuck in her throat.

Alan stretched his arms across the table and took her hands.

'Jenny,' he said. 'Will you marry me?'

Tears ran down Jenny's cheeks.

'Oh Alan, you utter pig!' she wept. 'Of course I will!'

* * *

Late that winter afternoon the two lovers strolled together along the Embankment, too happy to speak. They paused awhile and leant their arms on the parapet, watching the lamplight gleaming on the water. The river looked poetic and mysterious. Then Jenny asked the question that all lovers ask each other.

'When did you fall in love with me?'

'Right from the beginning I think, when I saw you in that blue dress, standing by the fountain, but I didn't really admit it to myself until that moment in the hospital when you bent over me in that white hospital gown, and kissed me. I though I'd died in heaven and an angel was kissing me.'

'Then why on earth did you keep me waiting all that time, supposing you had forgotten me?'

'Because I had nothing to offer you and you said you wanted to marry a millionaire. I had to concentrate desperately hard to amass enough wealth to dare approach you.'

'Now I know you're daft,' said Jenny, laughing at this image of herself as a haughty damsel who had to be wooed with rich gifts. 'As a matter of fact I finally fell for you when I saw you lying in the hospital so wan and woebegone, looking like a lonely little boy.'

'The fire must have been a blessing in disguise,' said Alan. 'I knew witchery was in the air when the ghosts of Embury started to walk.'

'The lightning must have set both our hearts ablaze,' said Jenny.

'And the fire will never go out,' said Alan, drawing her closer to him.

That promise they sealed with a long kiss.

When this betrothal embrace was over, Jenny sighed happily and laid her head on Alan's shoulder.

'We'll be married at the very first possible moment,' he said. 'And spend our honeymoon touring England until we find our own Embury.'